Africa Zero

Africa Zero

Neal Asher

Cosmos Books, an imprint of **Wildside Press**
New Jersey . New York . California . Ohio

Africa Zero

Published by:

Cosmos Books, an imprint of Wildside Press
P.O. Box 45, Gillette, NJ 07933-0045
www.wildsidepress.com

For more information, contact Wildside Press.

ISBN: 1-58715-447-1

Part 1

As the sun sunk behind the horizon I gathered lumps of bark from a huge preconvulsion baobab dying a hundred year death on the cliff top. By the time I had a fire going the moon was filling the night with mercury light, reflected from its labyrinth etched face, and hyraxes were screeching like murder victims from the heather trees behind me. It was for comfort really, the fire; for that old comfort born in the hidden psyche when men crouched in caves and feared the night, the last time the ice was here. I had no need of the heat or of cooked food. Few Earthly extremes of temperature were dangerous to me and the sustenance I took was poison to flesh.

While staring into the flames I slowly altered the spectrum of my hearing. The screeching of the hyraxes became a low gasping and other sounds began to impinge; the mutter of cooling rock and the strained whispering of the heather trees. Then, then a sound I had not heard in twenty years; the low infrasonic rumbles that were the conversation of mammoth. I listened for a while and realised I was smiling, then I stood from my fire, walked to the baobab at the edge of the Break and looked out over the silvered foothills.

Behind me the Atlas Mountains of Old Morocco still held back the ice that had swamped Europe. Six centuries in the past the hills below me had been bare, and arid where they faded into the Sahara desert. Five centuries ago the wasteland had begun to bloom as water vapour, blown down off the ice, condensed and fell in storms still told of around the campfires of bushmen. Now the hills were thick with vegetation, and wild with the fauna that fed on it including, of course, the mammoth. But it was not the ice that had caused their return.

Far below me a lone bull was tusking bark from a huge groundsel tree and muttering to himself like a grouchy old man. I watched him for a while and felt an affinity with those men in ancient Siberia to whom this creature had been all life and a lord of death, and who had hunted it to extinction. Men not so different from he who had resurrected it. I remembered the first herd; cloned from ten thousand years old carcases preserved in the Siberian tundra, gestated in the wombs of elephants, and kept as a tourist attraction in a national park in North Africa. Perhaps they would have remained no more than that; a novelty. But then had come the thinning of the human race.

To begin with, the compulsory sterilization of one in three people was introduced planet-wide. Then air transmitted HIV's and more virulent diseases had appeared. It was open to conjecture whether they had evolved or been manufactured. The nightmarish creatures that appeared and fed on the out-of-control third-world population had certainly been gene-spliced. The dictums at that time had been: Better not to be born than to be born and starve to death. Your neighbour dies so you might live. The human race cannot be strong while the weak breed: the human race must be prey. Some called it a catastrophe and against the teaching of God. Others called it the choice of survival.

During the chaos of that time, as ten billion people fought for insufficient resources and the encroaching ice sucked the planet dry, during the water wars, plagues, brief atomic conflicts, and desperate strivings to become established beyond Earth, the mammoth had broken free and roamed across North Africa. While millions then billions of humans died the mammoth burgeoned. I always considered this a beautiful irony and a kind of justice: humans had been too busy killing each other to notice. But then it is easy for me to make such judgements. I ceased to be human in many ways over two thousand years ago.

In time the bull finished with the tree and dozed in the moonlight with his four metre tusks resting on the ground. I turned away to head back for my fire, but then, suddenly, his trumpeting shattered the night. As the hyraxes fell silent I turned back to the Break. Something . . . something of flickering silver and shadow darted round him then was gone before I could upgrade my vision. Pykani? I doubted it. They would be in the air; dark bat shapes singing their calming songs as they moved in for blood. They would not have startled him. I waited and watched his heat and the red colours, but the shape did not reappear. At length I returned to my fire, troubled, but not unduly so.

* * *

The bright flames flickered and died like night spectres and the bark collapsed to black edged rubies. I considered the possibility of sleep and rejected it. I had slept for three hours a couple of days ago up on the ice and I would not need to sleep again for several weeks. Boredom drove me into fugue and I listened like a yogi to the oh so accurate ticking of my body clock as the altered moon traversed its arc and the hyraxes raised Cain. An hour before sunrise the sky began to lighten. Only then did I come out of fugue and kick dirt over the cooling ashes of my fire. Time to move on.

* * *

The Break was a new addition to the Atlas mountains. When the ice had first reached the coast of Old Morocco it was as if it had suddenly rested its entire weight there and tipped a plate on which the mountains rested. The event was The Convulsion and The Break was the further edge of that plate. It was heaved from the Atlas foothills in less than a year, seven centuries ago.

Under the baobab I removed my boots and put them in my pack. Then I removed the synthiflesh coverings of my fingers and toes and placed them in my pack as well. The sky was lighter then, pink tinted to the east, and that light glinted like blood off the knurling on the inner faces of my metal fingers; a reminder of what I am and what I am not. Shouldering my pack I moved to the edge, lowered myself over, and began to descend, driving my fingers and toes like pitons into the mossy crevices in the rock. At first I was careful. Even for me a fall from such a height could kill. As the sun breached the horizon I was two hundred feet down with another hundred to go. One bad moment then when a huge black scorpion did its damnedest to sting my face and I jerked away pulling a slab from the cliff face and abruptly found myself hanging by one hand watching the slab crash into the jungle below. Synthetic or not my reactions are still flesh, much to my chagrin. Fifty feet from the ground and I was scrabbling down the cliff face like a spider. I dropped the last twenty feet straight into the rosette of a giant lobelia, scattering sunbirds like a treasure of sapphires and emeralds. Once free of the flattened plant it took me some time to clean the sap from myself before I could replace my coverings and return to a semblance of humanity. Then, booted and fingered again, I made my way into the greenery.

Beyond the patch of lobelias, I pushed my way through a five-foot thicket of putrescent-smelling plants I could not put a name to, but these thinned out to give way to wild banana plants, groundsels hung with sulphurous yellow lichen, and a ground covering of bracken. Soon I reached the remains of the groundsel, of which the mammoth had made a meal, and there, where the jungle had been flattened, found progress easier. All around this area frogs were chirruping noisily, perhaps because they could now see the venomous spiders that hunted them. As I advanced, a python the thickness of my torso observed me speculatively from a tree, tested my scent with his tongue, then lost interest. At one point I heard something stalking me, but it soon went away. I was exposed on that narrow path, but I knew that if I stayed with the mammoth I would eventually encounter those I had come to see.

* * *

I smelt it an hour before I found it. The smells were not of carrion. The corpse was too fresh to have decayed. They were the smells of the blood and broken intestines of a huge ruminant. It was the bull I had seen the night before.

Three lions were feeding in a desultory manner while other scavengers were squabbling for their share. A mortuary of vultures held raucous autopsy; over their black feather suits their gory heads were hooked like question marks as they shrugged 'don't knows' at each other, then 'what the hells?' as they tipped them back to swallow choice bloody morsels. A pack of hyenas yipped and snarled round a leg that had been torn away. It must have taken the whole pack of them to drag the joint to where it lay, and from where they kept a wary eye on the lions, but there was plenty for all it would seem, else the lions would have been driven away. Other birds, small foxes, wild dogs, and feral cats had homed in on the bounty. Even a group of black skinned frogs had crawled from the undergrowth to lap at a pool of blood.

Leaning against the trunk of a vine choked baobab I switched off my sense of smell, but even then I could taste the blood in the air. It was a grisly scene. I looked at the lions and did not believe their claim. Three lions did not bring down and dismember something weighing nigh on thirty tons. Three lions did not shatter four-metre long tusks and break open a skull ten centimetres thick. I looked at the carnage with a clinical eye. I knew of only a few things that could do this; a roving tyrannosaur, but they were rare on the ground now as they tended to chase after people and end up on the wrong end of a missile launcher, and anyway, it would still have been feeding; the Chuthrat Dragon, which I knew to be on another continent; or man. This looked like the work of man. It looked as if a human being had taken out this mammoth with something like a laser. I advanced to hold my own autopsy.

Snarling, the hyenas moved out of my way then closed back in on their meat once I was past. One of the lions was not so obliging. It climbed to its feet, its stomach bulging ridiculously, and growled a warning at me. I continued my advance knowing that if I attempted to circle, it would probably move in front of me out of pure contrariness. As I drew closer, it stooped down and shuffled its back legs in preparedness to pounce. I timed my move carefully, knowing full stomach or not a lion can move with devastating alacrity. Snarling, it sprang straight at me; claws and teeth and a trail of bloody saliva. I stepped aside and caught it a blow on the shoulder, not too hard, just enough to send it cartwheeling through the air with a startled howl. It hit the ground and was up in an instant, its tail thrashing from side to side, then with clumsy dignity it retreated and watched me. Its two fellows, I noted, had been closing in from the sides and now pulled back, one to flop down panting, the other to clean itself conspicuously.

Once by the head of the mammoth I ignored the lions as I unshouldered my backpack and took off my shirt. The skull, I noted, was split cleanly, and the tusks had been sheared as if with a saw. Their faces looked almost polished. I pulled the two gory halves of the skull apart and probed around inside for shrapnel or the remains of some other projectile. I found none. I then inspected the outside of the head for sign of burning or at least singeing. No sign. I stepped further back, blood up my arms and across my chest, and tried to determine by the angle of fall, the surroundings, something, anything.

"Hold it right there, you bastard!"

I turned slowly. A woman stood about twenty feet from me. She was white, which was a surprise, had cropped blond hair, and was dressed in one of those grey, practically indestructible, monofilament coveralls. From this I deduced she must be a member of one of the corporate families that had come down to Africa during the Great Migration. For a moment I also thought she might be like me. Her right hand was of metal, tungsten ceramal like my own, but without a synthiflesh covering. But taking into account she held her rifle left handed I guessed that the hand might be all that was synthetic about her.

"I've been waiting for this for a long time," she said viciously.

"And what might that be?" I asked, relieved as I studied her weapon. It was not the disintegrator I had first assumed it to be. A pulse of antiphotons will do to me what it does to all matter. What she held was a projectile weapon, though admittedly a high tech one.

"You," she replied.

I considered that for a moment: either she knew who I was and had a grudge, in which case she had been very stupid to come after me with such inferior armament, or her assumptions were mistaken.

"I did not kill this mammoth," I said.

"Hah!" It was not even a laugh. "I saw you bat that lion aside. What have you got? Cybernetic implants? Is that what you used on the mammoth? Or is that too close in for you? What did you use, a ten mil flack rifle?"

I did not particularly admire her logic. "I restate. I did not kill this mammoth." I turned to fetch my shirt and pack.

"Hold it!"

I began to get annoyed. "Madam, either you are going to shoot or not. I tire of this ridiculous megalomaniacal badinage. What is it to be?" By this time I had turned side on to her and was ready to move.

"Wait," she sounded unsure now, but the rifle did not waver.

"You are—" I began, then mid-sentence I was springing sideways. Her gun flashed. There was surprisingly little concussion at her end, but half a metre from my left shoulder a proximity-shell burst and I felt lumps of shrapnel impacting on my skeleton. Then I was heading straight at her. She re-aimed. I moved aside again and the shell went off somewhere behind me. Then I was on her. I brought her down, knocked the rifle away, then caught her right arm as it raked for my face like a grapple. In that moment my eye-shutters clicked down. Her expression became one of angered horror. I saw it through a grid. My eyes were then mirrored spheres. As the inferior motors of her arm whined in protest at my grip and she battered at me ineffectually with her left fist of flesh I considered what to do next. Normally my reaction to threat is to kill its source, but she had been genuinely concerned about the mammoth, and for that I decided to be forgiving. I stood and hoisted her to her feet. She continued to struggle and then kicked me in the synthiflesh genitals.

When I showed no reaction she slumped, panting, and watched me warily.

"I experience no pain," I said, and the storm shutters came up, "but I can be damaged aesthetically." I then considered releasing her and in that moment the motors of her arm whined loudly. Obviously I had not been getting through to her. She would get it in a moment. I remained still. She continued to struggle for a moment, a mad look on her face, then she looked down at her wrist in disbelief. The penny dropped. She ceased to struggle.

"Please, do not kill Jethro Susan," came a lisping voice from nearby.

I looked round, then up at a dark form crouching on one of the stunted boughs of the baobab. The shape opened out and launched with a silent flap of its batlike wings and dropped down to my right. A Pykani; mahogany black leaning to translucence, a childlike body, shaped orange hair, and the white tips of fangs projecting over her bottom lip. She folded her wings on landing and made a curious warding gesture towards the felled mammoth.

"I consider a serious attempt on my life fair reason to kill the one who makes that attempt," I said, testing.

The Pykani advanced until she was looking up at me. "But as we both well know, no-one has made a serious attempt on your life in many hundreds of years, Collector."

"Spitfire," I said, recognising this Pykani and incidentally noting the look of shock appear on Jethro Susan's face.

"Will you release Jethro Susan?"

I looked at the woman. "As long as she promises to make no further attempt on me." She nodded. I released her. She glanced to where her gun lay and decided, prudently, to leave it there.

"That's why I couldn't break your grip," she said.

I nodded. "Yes, your arm is necessarily limited by its anchorages. The force required only to match mine would have ripped it from your body." I looked at her closely. "I presume it is only your arm that is synthetic?"

She shook her head. "Most of the right hand side of my torso," she touched her breast self-consciously, "and my right leg below the knee."

I turned to Spitfire. "You sent for me."

"Yes," said the Pykani, "and you have come, Collector."

"Someone, or something, is killing the mammoth," I stated.

Spitfire flared her wings and made that warding gesture again. "Let us leave this place of death and I will tell you woes, Collector."

I turned away and headed back to the mammoth to get my shirt and pack. When I returned to them Jethro Susan had retrieved her rifle and shouldered a pack of her own.

"Come south. We will await you, Collector and Jethro Susan," said Spitfire, and with that she launched herself into the air and soon was out of sight. Jethro Susan eyed me nervously.

"I have heard of you," she said by way of understatement.

"Hardly unusual," I said and proceeded to wipe drying gore from my arms and chest with handfuls of moss.

"I apologise for the mistake I made."

"Accepted."

"Why am I still alive?"

I considered that, wondering just what she had heard about me. I decided to answer her honestly.

"You are alive because your threat to me was out of anger for the mammoth and because I managed to disarm you before you could cause me further damage. Had I a weapon you would have been dead. Had your motives been otherwise you would have been dead."

"Clear enough," she said, her face white.

I thought then how difficult it must be for mere mortals to meet a living legend and hated myself for the conceit. After wiping myself down as best I could I inspected myself and decided it was not enough, and folded my shirt and put it in my pack before hoisting my pack onto my shoulder. I do adhere to a certain regimen of personal cleanliness, and this time, even though I had not used my synthetic sweat-glands or stomach for some time, there was the smell of putrefying blood to consider.

"Shall we?" I said, gesturing to the south. And so we set out, leaving the vultures and hyenas to their quarrelsome feeding.

Once away from the blood trampled clearing I glanced at the companion I had acquired.

"Jethro Susan . . . I take it you are from one of the corporate families?"

She looked at me with a kind of wary awe I found both endearing and annoying.

"Yes, the Jethro Manx Canard Combine."

"What brings you out here?"

She looked at the gleaming claw of her hand. "Ten years ago I was involved in an inter-family conflict. I got caught on the edge of an explosion. I had to be rebuilt like this because it seems that the boosted immune system I have makes it nearly impossible for my body to accept grafting. JMCC members are noted for physical perfection. I became a pariah."

I glanced at her again, wondering if she was lying.

"Surely your body will accept grafts of its own tissue, vat-grown limbs and the like?"

"No," she shook her head, "my immune system was boosted to cope with doppleganger parasites. Apparently, as I grew up my tissue was marked in some way, the genome itself . . . that mark is impossible to find let alone transcribe, what with selfish DNA there to blur matters."

Not her words, but the look of bitter anger on her face, told me she was not lying. Her words gave me pause though. Had things gone so far downhill?

"Ah, at least you have some body," I said by way of consolation. Not something I am very good at.

She looked at me. "For a moment I forgot . . . Collector." She seemed to find the honorific difficult. "Your entire body, but for your brain and some nerve tissue is . . . manufactured."

"Fair bit of that as well. It's held in a mutating super-conductor web at zero K and connected into various sensory sub systems."

"If you don't mind me asking . . . How old are you?"

"I do mind."

Which killed that conversation stone dead. I guess we are all sensitive about something.

Part 2

Hours of walking and pushing through tangled growth brought us to another clearing and the flicker of a fire in evening light. Three of the Pykani were cooking food that I assumed was for Jethro Susan. I squatted by the flames and removed my pack. She slumped by the fire nearer to the Pykani than to me. She looked exhausted. Only then did I realise how she must have struggled to keep with the pace I naturally set. I looked across at Spitfire.

"Have you water?"

The Pykani stood, took up a gourd, and handed it to me. I washed out my mouth with some then proceeded to wash the dried blood from my arms, my torso, and from under my fingernails. Only when I had finished that and was pulling pieces of shrapnel from my shoulder did anyone speak.

"You have come," said the Pykani next to Spitfire, who I recognised as her mate.

"Yes," I said, trying to remember his name. Had it been Hurricane? "How many mammoth have been killed?"

"At our last census it was seven hundred this way. Twenty five by other methods."

At that moment I remembered to turn my sense of smell back on and with it came a flush of anger; redolent of fire smoke and the roasted mammoth flesh Jethro Susan was eating.

"What more can you tell me?"

"The Silver One has been seen."

I closed my eyes. And it comes to this: the obligations of life eternal.

"I will find . . . that one," I said.

Jethro Susan looked from the Pykani to me in confusion, but I felt no urge to relieve her of it. As I said before, there are some things to which even I am sensitive. And there is old pain.

"The herds move south for the winter. I take it the killer moves with them?"

"Thus far," said Hurricane. Yes, it was Hurricane. I looked at Spitfire. "How long has this killing been going on?"

"This is the second year, Collector," she said, as wise in my ways as all the peoples of the plains, and not prepared to ask the questions she might. It was otherwise with Jethro Susan.

"This Silver One . . . I have heard of it."

I looked at her and looked away. The Pykani observed her as if embarrassed by her gaucherie, but I could see that they were eager to hear how I might reply to her. I decided to tell them a little of it.

"It is a call to me," I said, "I think, perhaps, in the end this is my responsibility. What more might call me than the killing of my mammoth?"

Jethro Susan looked at me calculatingly then down at her silver claw. I think it was then that she understood what the Silver One might be. The Pykani, there were four of them, two who remained silent, looked at me with burning eyes. They had caught the nuance: my mammoth. Again I looked at them, knowing they were owed an explanation.

"Why am I called Collector?" I asked.

An old, hairless Pykani, who until then had remained silent, was quick to answer. "You are called Collector because you collect the genetic heritage of those who might be driven extinct. You are the curator of species; saving what might be lost." He looked to Spitfire. "My daughter has told me how you bearded the Great African Vampire in his home on the ice and collected tissue from the birth that comes after from his mate."

I nodded. "It has always been my purpose to preserve life."

Jethro Susan looked at me as if I had just told them I was a giraffe. I smiled. "Yes, life, not individuals." I looked back at the Pykani. "Your myths are true. I tell you this because of your trust in me. It was I who stripped viable DNA from the corpses of mammoth taken from the Siberian tundra and made it whole enough to inject into the eggs of elephants."

With this they would have to be satisfied. I did not tell them that it was also I who spliced human DNA with that of the vampire bat to produce a people capable of utilising the reusable resource the mammoth represented, or that it was I who created the Great African Vampires to cull the human race. There is such a thing as too much knowledge. I looked to Jethro Susan and saw stunned awe registered on her face. I had answered one of her questions. She now had some idea of my age.

* * *

That night I sat and watched the stars as the mutilated face of the electric moon beamed down and Jethro Susan slept. Lost in philosophical thought I wondered how the face of that moon, changed so certainly by the human race, might affect the minds of all those born to see its light. It occurred to me then that I had seen changes I had not registered until that moment. Many people now, I felt, lived with a greater assurance of their position in the universe; a higher sense of worth and an acceptance of responsibility. I looked at the huddled form of Jethro Susan and realised I would have to acknowledge this and that I could not just march south now as arbitrary judge and executioner. For the sake of humanity, at last, I would have to delegate some of the responsibility and accept a companion. That decision made I stared at the far stars until morning, guessing what wonders unfolded in the colonies.

* * *

The bloody, hung-over eye of time breached the horizon to a strident chorus of black frogs. Knowing human frailty well, but distantly, I waited for Jethro Susan to wake. While I waited, the Pykani returned from a night's feeding and flying. Shortly after they arrived, greeted me, then went to doze in the groundsels, Jethro Susan thrashed in her sleep and grabbed at her ceramal hand as if it were a source of torment to her, then she woke.

She jerked and rolled over, staring at the mossy ground as her breathing quickened with her wakening. I watched her as she coughed and spat and pushed herself upright, and I felt a pang of something half forgotten, something human. Bleary-eyed, she took up a gourd, drank, then looked at me.

"Do you never sleep?" she asked me.

"Infrequently," I replied, then, "do you wish to come with me?" I was anxious, now that the night had passed, to be on my way.

She shook her head as if dispelling cobwebs before replying. "I had hoped as much. Would I delay you?"

I considered that. Every moment of delay would mean more dead mammoth, yet I estimated the mammoth population to be over a hundred thousand, so they were in no danger of extinction, though I knew that what killed them could eventually bring them to it.

"Responsibility," I said, and it was a key word. I let it rest there for a moment, but I could see she did not understand me.

"Do you think I am responsible?" she asked.

"No, but you are human."

Again she looked at me in confusion. I suppose it was a bit unfair of me. I had all but forgotten things like aching muscles, blood sugar levels, and a full bladder. I said to her, "I saw the human race reach its limit, on this planet, of twelve billion, and the hell that produced. I saw them step into space as a last resort, before collapse, and save themselves. I watched the space habitats being built and the bases on the moon. I travelled to Mars and watched Phobos and Deimos being ignited for the great terraforming project, and I saw the seed-ships set out for the far stars. Forty or more colonies now thrive at distances from us that are unimaginable and Earth has become a backwater. I say to you that the nigh immortality of the human race is assured. But I ask you: is that the limit of our responsibility? That we survive? No. I say no. I say that as survival becomes much more easy for us we should take on responsibility for others not of our genome."

"The mammoth," said Jethro Susan, standing up, then, "I need a piss." And she wandered into the jungle leaving me sitting there embarrassed by my pomposity. Shortly she returned.

"You know, that's really easy for you to say. For everyone it is their own survival which is of most importance. You, of course, can take this moral high ground because survival for you is so easy."

She had me there. There was no getting away from it. I could have stood up then and gone my and done what I had to do and in a century or so she would have been so much decaying matter. Then, for reasons other than my purported morals, I decided I wanted her as a companion. I saw that here was a woman who might counter the greatest threat to my life, which was boredom.

Jethro Susan breakfasted on cold mammoth meat while I looked on. When she was finished she took up her pack and looked at me in readiness.

"We follow the trails of the herds south to the plains," I said, standing also and taking up my pack.

* * *

And so we set out, with me leading the way, pushing through the jungle until we crossed a mammoth trail as wide as a three lane motorway, where the chewed remains of cycads littered the crushed vines, and where hundredweight piles of dung swarmed with busy scarab beetles. We left the Pykani dozing in the trees, but that night they came to speak with me and play a game with red seeds on a gridwork board while Jethro Susan slept. As we played and talked I wondered how rationalized my reasons were for allowing her along and what the Pykani thought of my delaying for her. That night I asked Spitfire.

"It is our wish that you keep Jethro Susan with you."

I was surprised, though I should not have been, obviously there was some sort of bond here. I waited. Spitfire continued. "She is sworn to the herd and we have braided debt with her. We wish her the opportunity to repay."

"Only those who partake of the sustenance can be sworn to the herd. She drinks blood?"

"It is so. We saw her when she had left JMCC. She was being hunted by the GAV himself and had not time to hunt for herself. She ran far and craftily while we watched and nearly killed the GAV with her rifle. He gave up on her for easier prey to the east. She could barely walk by then, but she still had her rifle, and then she came upon one of the little Thunderers."

Hurricane took up the dialogue. "She raised her rifle and we were ready to fall on her, but she did not shoot. She lowered her rifle and told the little one to go in peace. Then she collapsed."

I nodded; so and thus, at the edge of starvation she had refused to kill one of the baby mammoth for meat. I wondered why. In such a situation I would have killed, but the point was moot.

"We came to her then and she was as weak as a fledgling. We gave her the fledgling's drink. The blood of Thunderers restored her."

I winced at that; regurgitated blood.

"Hence her swearing to the herd," I said. I looked to where she lay. She was awake, I could tell, but she did not move. "How did the debt become braided?"

"Twice now she has led corporate hunts astray. Once she killed one of her own to prevent him killing. And we saved her from pursuit by driving an old bull to stamp a JMCC ground car."

I smiled and wondered just how long she had been with the Pykani. I had seen stranger matches.

* * *

On our third night-time stop Spitfire and her father flew in with news for us just as Jethro Susan was bedding herself down. They swept in, to land in a small clearing next to the one we had made for the fire, and with their eyes averted, they approached. I gathered it was their intention to be off again, else they would have been more sociable. But they were nocturnal by nature and did not want to ruin their night vision with the light of the fire.

"What is it?" I asked, expecting news of more dead mammoth.

"The herds move to the east," said Spitfire.

I waited.

Her father said, "In the east there are large cycads and by going there they miss difficult terrain. It has always been so."

"We'll follow their trail, as we have been."

Spitfire shook her head regretfully. "In a few days they will turn to the west again then resume their course to the south."

I began to entertain a nasty suspicion. "This difficult terrain they are avoiding. Would it have a name by any chance?"

Spitfire and her father looked at each other, each waiting for the other to speak. It was Jethro Susan who spoke.

"Z'gora." She said it like a curse.

The name was familiar.

"Z'gora . . . Z'gora . . ." Then I remembered. "The Zag people. They're the ones with some unusual pets. I got a sample there about fifty years ago. Don't they have some nasty habits?"

Spitfire and her father made quick warding gestures.

Jethro Susan said, "If we went through Z'gora we could make up a day, perhaps more . . ."

I looked at her. "I know I should not ask this, but are you up to it?"

She snorted contemptuously and tapped the side of her rifle.
"I've been through there before. They're easy enough to handle.
You just don't let them get too close."

"Very well then. We go through Z'gora."

Spitfire and her father moved away from the fire and took off
into the night.

"When will we get there?" I asked.

"Midday tomorrow," said Jethro Susan, and rolled herself up
in her blanket.

I sat through the rest of the night with the patience of a machine.

* * *

In the morning Jethro Susan climbed an ambatch tree to take
sightings back from the Atlas Mountains, and from some
mountains she said should be to the southeast of us. Once she
had scrambled back to the ground again she looked at her compass and pointed to a wall of jungle to our right.

"That way," she said, then removed her pack and dropped it
on the ground. I wondered what she was doing for a moment
until she removed a formidable looking panga.

"You carry my pack. I'll start."

I let her lead on. I picked up her pack and followed. She was
being foolish, and I think perhaps she realised this, but she was a
stubborn woman with a point to prove. She started on the wall
of jungle as if it had offered her personal affront. For two hours
she hacked a path for us before she started to show any signs of
slowing. Of course it was not her arm that was tiring, but the rest
of her musculature; the part of her that was flesh. I let her go at it
for another hour before I called a halt.

"Okay, I'll take over now," I said.

Jethro Susan turned and looked at me as if suspecting me of
sarcasm. There was none to find. I took the panga from her and
handed her our packs. I tried not to let the next few hours look
easy for me, but I guess what gave it away was my lack of sweat.
When we broke through into thinner growth we could push
through I handed her panga back and congratulated her on its
keenness. She accepted it with a look of annoyance and threw
my pack at me. I caught it and put it on.

At midday we had not reached Z'gora as predicted and we
halted so Jethro Susan could rest. I took the opportunity to do

some scouting. We were close to the Zag peoples and some of them might be about.

"I'm just going for a look around."

Jethro Susan rubbed at her shoulder and nodded acquiescence. I left my pack by her and moved off into the jungle as quietly as I could. It is surprising how quietly you can move when you have accumulated decades of experience, and when there are no fatigue poisons in you, and no lungs. I circled our stopping place looking for signs of movement. Like Jethro Susan I climbed a couple of trees. As I crept back I saw Jethro Susan sitting on a log rummaging through her pack. I moved very quietly, not for her sake, but for the man decked out in feathers and dyed hyrax skins who was creeping up behind her.

I got to about three feet behind him when he was the same distance behind her. He raised a wooden spike with a suspicious looking green tarry substance on it. I tapped him on the shoulder.

"Excuse me."

He yelled. Jethro Susan yelled and fell off her log. Annoyed, because he had passed me without me seeing him, I broke his neck.

"Jesu!"

Jethro Susan came up from behind the log with leaves in her hair and in her mouth. She spat them out and looked down at the man. Then she looked at me with annoyance.

"Did you have to make him yell like that?"

I could not help it. She had fallen off the log and there she was with leaves in her hair asking questions like that. I started chuckling. Her look of disbelief turned that into a laugh. I just stood there and laughed.

"You're a monster!" she said.

"Oh dear," I said, shaking my head and gradually getting myself under control. Still grinning I stooped down and picked up the wooden spike the man had been carrying. Then I drove it into the log in front of her.

"I remember now," I said, "that tarry substance is a derivative of curare. It will leave you paralysed but it won't kill you. They like to keep their prey fresh."

Jethro Susan looked at the spike in horror. I picked up the Zag tribesman by his broken neck and tossed him up into the forked branch of a nearby acacia. Let him serve as a warning. Or was I just being melodramatic?

Two hours of travel across relatively easy terrain from our rest site and first encounter with the Zag we came out on an open hill top and looked down on Z'gora. It had once been a city of the third millennium, only the name had been different then. It had been called New Babylon in defiance of all that was Western. To the right of it was a wide flat area on which very little grew. From there, a thousand years in the past, had been launched the vanguard of the African space effort. The buildings of the city still stood, but now they were over-grown with vines and dwelt in by primitives. Jethro Susan and I found a path down into it and proceeded with caution.

We were about a hundred metres from the first building when I heard them. I turned to Jethro Susan.

"Put your hood up and keep your head low, they're here."

She did as instructed.

"Last time I came through I let off a couple of shots and they kept away from me," she said.

I said, "The last time I was here I snapped a few necks and they kept away. But as I well know, people are never predictable. Have you any gloves?"

She unfurled a glove from a pouch pocket on her sleeve and put it on her hand of flesh.

"Keep your head down," I said as we advanced.

As we moved down into the city I saw that we might soon be in trouble, or rather, Jethro Susan might. Trees encroached on the path down there and made adequate cover for an ambush. I looked around on the ground and found a couple of rocks.

"Put a couple of shots into those trees, that might deter them," I said.

Obligingly Jethro Susan unhitched her rifle and put a shot in the trees each side of the path. Two concussions blew burning foliage into the air. There was some shouting and the sound of running feet, then silence. As we drew closer to the trees I thought it might have worked, then something thudded in the side of my neck. I reached up and pulled out a feathered thorn just as another bounced off Jethro Susan's monofilament hood. I saw movement in the bushes and threw a rock. There was a soggy thud and a cry of pain. Just then Jethro Susan's rifle cracked and there was an explosion above. A feathered man fell out of the trees with all the aerodynamics of a brick. He hit the path and bounced, a hole where his chest used to be. I heard running feet, retreating.

"Stragglers," I told her.

There were no more attacks from the trees.

We entered the city with a degree of caution and stayed at the centre of the streets. A man showed himself at a window and Jethro Susan loosed another shot. The explosion lit the inside of a room. There was a horrible creaking, then a large lump of vine choked wall fell crashing to the ground. Pieces of stone bounced past us.

"Save your shots or we'll have the lot down on us. Building inspectors would have nightmares about this place."

I noticed that under her hood she was grinning.

Halfway into the city and with no more shots fired, the natives began to show themselves. In a doorway we saw a naked child of about four with a huge preying mantis crouching on his shoulder. He was petting it. Jethro Susan shuddered.

"You were right about the unusual pets. I never saw them before. I was moving fairly quickly though."

I considered that.

"It might be an idea if we did that now. You never know what they might be planning. Your monofilament gear might stop darts but it won't stop an arrow or a spear."

We broke into a trot, turned down a side street leading in the direction we wanted to go. Behind us there was more movement as people began to come out of their ancient homes.

"Faster," I said, and we began to run. Ahead of us I could smell wood smoke and wondered if it was something they were preparing for us. Soon we rounded a corner and came face to face with about twenty Zag tribesmen, women, and children. It seemed we had stumbled in one some kind of celebratory feast. On spits, over the fire, were the gutted corpses of four men. The air smelt of roast pork.

"Jesu!" said my companion at the sight.

We came to a halt. Those in front of us did not look as if they had any intention of moving. Others were gathering behind. The situation was beginning to look decidedly sticky. I would have survived it. I am not so sure Jethro Susan would have.

"Look!" I shouted, and held up my arms.

Jethro Susan looked at me as if she thought me mad. I guess she wanted to start shooting about then. I shook my head at her.

The Zags were watching me closely now. I lowered my hands to my neck and pressed my fingers to a sequence of soft spots, then I sent an internal signal to a number of superconductor nerve nexuses. My face went numb as seals broke and fibres and synthetic muscle autodetached.

"Look!" I shouted again, and when I was absolutely sure I had their attention I pulled my face off.

To say that the effect was electric would be an understatement. Just about all of them screamed. Jethro Susan only just managed to stifle her's. About half of them ran for it. A lot went face down on the concrete. The remainder stood there with their mouths open and just stared. I looked behind and got a similar reaction there. By this time Jethro Susan was getting the idea. She held her hand of ceramal high and pulled back her sleeve to show the rest of her arm. Like showmen we advanced then and none barred our way. One gawper reached out to try and touch my head as I passed but I slapped his hand away and grinned at him, which at that moment was all I was capable of doing.

Soon we reached a clear street, broke into a run, and in a matter of minutes were out on the plain of the landing field. There we stopped while I put my face back on.

"You ever pull a stunt like that again . . ."

I looked at Jethro Susan and noticed how white her complexion was. She did not look very well.

As the seals pulled down and the fibres reattached, feeling returned to my face, and I managed a normal looking smile.

"I'll try my best, but it was all I could think of at the time. It worked well, didn't it?"

Angrily she pulled her hood back, took off her remaining glove, and went stomping off to the south. I shrugged and followed on. That night we continued walking and did not make camp until we were well away from Z'gora. Jethro Susan was not very talkative. I guess it must be unnerving to see the true nature of things. But as she was settling down for the night her curiosity got the better of her.

"Doesn't it bother you being . . . what you are?" she asked me from her blankets.

"You mean, does it bother me that I have a wider sensorium that any man, hyperstrength, and am virtually immortal, then no, it doesn't bother me."

"That's not what I mean, and you know it."

I grinned, but in the darkness I doubted if she could see me.

I said, "Tell me, why do you not have a synthiflesh covering on your hand and arm? Such could be easily manufactured at JMCC, and once linked in to your nervous system it is almost as

sensitive as normal flesh. Could it be you were making a statement to your fellows? `Here, I have lost my arm. I am physically
imperfect. Look at me.' Rubbing their noses in it a bit, weren't
you?"

"You're getting away from the point," she said angrily.

"Ah, so you don't like personal questions either."

She was silent for a while, then she said, "You're right. I was
rubbing their noses in it. My imperfections were not my fault.
What right did they have to judge me by them?"

"What am I? Jethro Susan."

"A cyborg."

"A cyborg is something part machine and part human. Are
the proportions important? You should know."

"I see . . ."

"I'm human, Jethro Susan; I think and I feel. Yes, sometimes
it bothers me how I appear to others. But overall I feel the advantages outweigh the disadvantages. I think, it would be better
if you asked these questions of yourself."

There was a long silence then, but I knew she had not gone to
sleep. Eventually she asked another question.

"Are you? Are you really human?"

"Go to sleep, Jethro Susan."

Part 3

On the fifth day we left our camp of the night and headed toward the distant sound of vultures squabbling. I was sure of what we would find. Half an hour's walk brought to us the stink of putrefaction. An hour's walk brought us to the slaughtered carcase of a young female mammoth.

I held myself at the edge of the trampled clearing and watched as a pack of wild dogs fed. At my side Jethro Susan pulled the cloth from her mouth then swore and spat in a most crude manner. I moved to inspect the kill but her hand on my arm halted me.

"One like you is killing them," she said, "I did not know there was another."

I turned to her. "There were many of us once, nigh indestructible, unkillable. In time some of us sought death because of ennui or despair. Those that did sought it from their own kind mostly, as being the only ones capable. I have been called." I turned to go, but she held onto me, staring into the clearing suspiciously. I said, "It is the curse of some that they must kill those things they loved." She released me, and just at that moment I heard it; the sighing whine, and the electric crackle of undergrowth exploding into flame. In one motion I caught Jethro Susan round the waist and leapt five metres into the jungle to one side. My shutters went down as there was a candent purple flash behind me and a gust of sparkling cinders. I dropped Jethro Susan.

"Hide," I said, and leapt again.

To my right I caught the nacreous glitter of the beam and dropped to the ground as it swept above me blowing a cycad to candent flinders. I ate dirt and felt real fear for the first time in decades. Someone had an antiphoton weapon. Someone was trying to kill me and could succeed. I could die.

I was up and running at full speed, circling the clearing, but trying to keep to cover which was rapidly being blown away. Trees disappeared like pillars of ash in a hurricane and red fire flashed through the undergrowth. I had an idea where it was coming from now and by another circuitous route headed that way. The firing stopped. I closed in, found the vine covered log used for shelter . . .

It rested against the log. It looked like a stubby carbine made out of glass and old wood. Under the glass salamanders writhed. For a moment I did not hear the high-pitched terminal whine, when I did, I turned and ran. In the clearing I saw Jethro Susan coming towards me with her rifle.

"Run!" I yelled. She ran. As I came up beside her I explained while she gasped for breath. I did not need to gasp. No part of me needed oxygen.

"Antiphoton rifle keyed to dump its load. About a kiloton."

She looked at me with horror.

"I'll have to carry you."

She nodded agreement. This was no time for silly arguments. She knew my capabilities. I dashed ahead of her, stopped and stooped down. In a moment she was on my back and I set out at increased speed.

"Christ!" she managed, before she got her head down.

In a moment I was up to thirty-five kilometres an hour, which is fast enough over such terrain. I was on the edge, clipping cycads and groundsels and only just maintaining my balance on the soft ground. Jethro Susan yelled as a branch tore her leg. Nothing I could do then. In a minute we were on to the three-lane swathe cut by the main herd. I accelerated, feeling heat build up in my joints because of the extra loading. I turned on my sweat glands, but there was no water in my gut to supply them. I swore. Forty kilometres an hour, forty five. I intended to keep this up for as long as possible. Flies spattered my face and the occasional small bird did not get out of my way quickly enough. Fifty, and I leapt a very shocked looking lioness. Jethro Susan was swearing unremittingly in my ear. Her legs and arms were wrapped round me vicelike. Then it hit.

The jungle whited out. I decelerated fast and got us behind a tree. Jethro Susan lay face down with her arms around her face and I lay atop her. My eye shutters adjusted to the glare and I saw the facing sides of trees and cycads smoking. The flash went as the sound hit; the sound of matter being destroyed, a sound without regard for animal frailty or softness, hard edged as broken glass. Then the air seemed to shift to one side. The pressure dropped, rose steeply, then a hurricane brought the jungle down on us like a wave.

It is only fair to say that every vital part of me is shielded against radiation. Should every shred of synthiflesh be burned from my body I would survive. I had been out of danger once we were on the trail. I am not flesh. Jethro Susan was.

The storm ended while the jungle burnt. An ash of burnt and burning leaves snowed down. Jethro Susan shifted under me and complained with muffled swearing about my weight. There was no water in me to supply my tear ducts. There were ashes in my mouth. She could complain as much as she liked, but she was dead, if not now then some time soon, about a thousand rads dead.

* * *

"Will you get off of me you great lump of scrap!"

She had managed to turn her head to one side. I obliged her, hauling her to her feet as well. She brushed dirt from her coverall, yelled then swore when a burning leaf touched her face, then unzipped the coverall's hood from a pocket at the back of her neck and pulled it up over her head.

After a moment she said, "I thought we'd lost the tech for those things. How come there was one here?"

If I choose for there to be no expression on my face there is none. I was glad of that ability then. She did not know.

"It was an old one. It would have fetched a small fortune at JMCC or one of the other family complexes. Over five hundred years old. Antique."

She looked round at the carnage.

"How dirty was that explosion?" she asked carefully.

"Pretty bad, we'll have to circle round."

I set out into the burning jungle with her trailing behind.

Pretty bad.

At some point I would have to tell her that the explosion we had been on the edge of was equivalent to that of a tactical neutron bomb. Even the jungle we were walking through was fatal. I led us out of the area as quickly as I could.

We made about ten miles before she started to vomit. Five miles more and she was vomiting bile turned pink with blood and staggering to keep up with me. I halted. She sat down abruptly and I saw that she was crying; her tears leaving dirty streaks down the powder of ash on her face.

"I don't want to die," she protested, her voice breaking.

It got to me. I realised then I had come to care for her. I did not want her to die, or rather, I was not indifferent. I unhitched my pack and took out my sampling and field study kit. She watched me as I took out a hand diagnosticer and ran it over her from head to foot. I might well have used a Geiger counter.

"How long have I got?"

One statement and one question that have dogged humanity for all their time. I loaded a hollow-beam injector with the few drugs I had that would help her.

"Five days at the outside, unless you get help."

I reached over, pulled back her hood. The injector sighed against her neck. She slumped immediately. Five days at the outside. With help she might live another five. I considered increasing the dosage so she would never wake up, and rejected the idea. A plan was forming; something I might attempt, and which had a strange kind of justice. Yes. My decision made I scooped her up and ran into the jungle heading southeast to where the JMCC complex lay under the harsh sun of the savannah.

Two days and one night brought me to the edge of the jungle and the beginning of a green sea of elephant grass ornamented with the occasional flat-topped acacia. Once this place had been called the Sahara desert, but like the Atlas foot hills it had bloomed.

I suspected I had outdistanced the Pykani because I saw no sign of them on that night of travel. After a further half day of travel through the grasses I had to search for a water hole for Susan and myself. I had kept her under for most of the time, only waking her to drink from her water bottle, which was now empty. I needed water because the extra loading, even at a fairly steady pace of twenty kilometres per hour, was causing me to overheat again. I needed to fill my gut and glands with it so I could sweat to cool. It took me the rest of the day to find the water hole, which lay in a concealed hollow below three huge baobabs like sentinels. I threw a blanket over Susan and left her to sleep and wake naturally so she could drink before we moved on. At the water's edge I filled her water bottle and myself, batting away curious turtles while I did so. This done I returned and settled down by her. While I waited I ran a diagnostic on myself. It was unlikely there was anything wrong, but it passed the time.

By evening Susan had not stirred and I was considering picking her up and moving on. As I reached for her a shriek echoed across the plain as if from the inner ring of Hell; part man, part bird, and part madness. It was distant, but I well knew it was not far enough away. The next shriek was closer, and shortly after that a dark shape occluded the stars and there was a booming as of sails caught in a wind. The shape descended to land on the central baobab. Again the shriek. I saw eyes glinting red madness and upgraded my vision. There he was; the Great African Vampire himself, last male of his kind unless the child I had heard being born two years back was a male as well. He was an impressive sight; a twelve-metre wing span, the body of a man crossed with a cat, claws like hook knives, feet of an eagle, and the bear-dog face with four-inch fangs trailing saliva. I observed him clinically as he folded his wings. He then spoke to me in that hissing voice, his tail cracking like a whip.

"I smell the moon's blood on her . . . machine."

"I am aware of the sharpness of your senses, vampire."

"She dying. Why concern yourself with her? You waste. Give her to me. I know her and she escaped me."

"I have your code. You are one of the last. It would pain me to kill you, but in this you are on dangerous ground."

"Feelings, machine?"

"Yes, feelings."

"I could take her from you."

"I never sleep, and I could break you like a handful of twigs. You know this."

That got the civilities out of the way. He settled down in the tree and was silent for a while. When he spoke again it was with less bravado.

"It was you I sought, machine."

Had he come to meet his maker? Perhaps he had found out. "Why?"

"I have a son. He grows strong and well and soon will leave to seek his own prey."

"I am glad for you," and I truly was.

He continued speaking, his red eyes glaring at me. "I think much, on the ice, and I read books. Once we were many. Many were killed by corporate families for bounty. I, my mate and my son are all, now. It is not enough. Who will mate with my son? A daughter? This makes . . . weakness."

I think it was the longest speech I had ever heard from him and I was surprised at his knowledge. I had genetic tissue taken from the afterbirth of his son and at any time, with equipment I had concealed all round the world, I could resurrect his race. From that piece of tissue I could artificially cause diversification and soon have a viable breeding population. He wanted to do it the old way. He wanted his family to continue. Perhaps he wanted to have grandchildren. A funny thought when applied to the monster in the baobab. A creature that tore the heads from human beings to drink their blood and lymph and some-times ate such delicacies as their livers, raw, of course.

"Why are you telling me this?"

"You are collector of genetic heritage, curator of species."

He had that verbatim from the Pykani.

"So?" said I.

"You are the Collector. You know."

I looked down at Susan and considered what I would be do-ing to the human race, once again. Susan was personal. This was about what I am. At that moment there was over a billion hu-man beings on Earth, and three Great African Vampires.

"You must select from as diverse a collection of humankind as you can; Negroid, Caucasian, Asian . . . The Pykani as well, as they were spliced from men."

His bear-dog face showed puzzlement. It was a comical sight.

"I do not understand."

"You too were spliced from humankind. It is possible for you to breed with them. It may just be that this way you can get a via-ble breeding population started."

He snarled. "They are prey."

"They are survival."

He shrieked and launched himself into the air, wings boom-ing, branches snapped from the baobab. I watched him go then turned to look down at Susan. She was awake and looking at me in horror.

"Come, let me help you to the water."

She did not want my help, but in the end had to accept it. As she drank her fill at the water hole I noted the sores breaking out on the back of her neck and the way her hair was beginning to fall out. She would have been poison to him.

* * *

The JMCC complex squatted on the plain like a huge metallic crab. It was five kilometres in diameter, but less than half a kilometre in height. Windows below the smooth dome of the roof glinted like beady eyes. Off to one side and partially hidden by the complex itself was the fenced-off landing field, a scattering of control towers, and a behemoth of a delta wing shuttle. To the people of Earth the corporate families were notoriously reclusive. This was only because they had no interest in Earth. Their interests were in the space above it. Holding Susan before me I slowed to a walk for the last few kilometres. I had about a kilometre to go when the ground car headed out to me.

The car was of a design I had not seen before, though similar in construction to ground cars used over a thousand years ago. It had rectangular body, with tinted windows all around, over six bulbous rubber-tyred wheels. I was surprised. Wheels? I could even hear the engine. Had things gone so far downhill? I wondered if my plans for Susan were any longer tenable. If they no longer used antigravity then perhaps other technologies had slid into the abyss.

It drew to a halt before me, doors hissed open, and three men in monofilament coveralls, which looked suspiciously like military uniforms, stepped out. Two of them were armed with hand-held machine guns. Primitive. The third had some kind of laser pistol holstered at his hip, which was more reassuring as far as my plans were concerned. The one with the laser spoke first.

"That woman is JMCC," he said. He seemed at a loss for anything to add.

"Yes, she is certainly that, and she is in need of medical attention." I began to walk forward. The machine pistols trained on me. I halted. They might hit Susan.

"What is wrong with her?"

"Are you a doctor?" He looked to his two companions. "You are not. Why then do you need to know what is wrong with her? That is out of your jurisdiction. Now kindly stop waving those toys about and take us into the complex." I began to walk again.

"Wait! . . ." He seemed confused.

I said, "I don't think Jethro Hendrickson would be too impressed with your behaviour. Now kindly stop fucking me about."

He looked to his companions then said slowly, "Thomas Canard is Chairman now . . . Jethro Hendrickson died over a hundred years ago . . . "

"So, I'm not up to date on your affairs. This woman is one of yours and she is dying."

He unhooked his radio from his belt and spoke into it in some sort of word code. After a pause to listen to the reply he asked me, "What is your name and status?" Should I lie? No. The truth would get things moving a lot more quickly.

"I am the Collector," I said.

Three faces abruptly lost their tan. The speaker dropped his hand to his laser pistol as if for reassurance and found none. After a pause he cleared his throat and spoke into the radio again. The voice that replied to him was a different voice, and not in code.

"Bring them in."

They brought us in.

Part Four

Things moved quickly once we were inside the complex. A medical team met the ground car in a place like an aeroplane hangar and Susan was soon laid out on a stretcher. A harassed looking doctor asked me about her condition. When I told him he shook his head morosely.

"If that's the case we can do little more than make her comfortable."

"What about superconductor gridding and flash freezing?"

He looked at me as if I needed some kind of medical attention myself. "S-con gridding and flash freezing? They're theoretically possible, I suppose."

When he said no more he and the other medics wheeled Susan away. I knew I would get no action at this level, so once they were gone I turned to the guards who were lingering around me and nervously fingering their weapons.

"I would like to see Thomas Canard if that is possible?" I was all politeness. It was not yet time to start breaking heads and ripping doors off their hinges. Later, perhaps.

The guard who had spoken to me outside looked incredibly relieved. "He wishes to see you. Please, come with me." I noticed he was being more polite. It is amazing what fear can do for social intercourse.

They led me from the hangar through baroquely decorated corridors. I noted with an amount of distaste and annoyance that some of those decorations consisted of trophies from GAVs. My annoyance was at myself for not considering this. Two years ago I could have come here for a tissue sample instead of crusading across the ice after a living vampire with an extremely nasty temper. The distaste was for the kind of mental attitudes that must have become prevalent in JMCC in the last century. Attitudes that made trophy hunting and near genocide acceptable. Had I been about then, this would not have happened. But I had been in China tracking down the Chuthrat Dragon. It had taken me thirty-six years to get that sample. By the time I heard what was going on back here most of the vampires had been exterminated. I then rushed back from China to get a vampire tissue sample. There had not seemed to be any need before. The GAVs had been doing quite nicely thank you.

Eventually we came to a turbo lift that shot us up to the top of the complex in less time than it took one of my guards to pick his nose. The doors swished open on luxurious apartments.

The walls were hung with paintings which to my knowledge had been there for six centuries. There were corporation emblems and arrays of polished weapons, some of them a lot better than the ones my guards were carrying. On pedestals there were various suits of body armour and one motorized exoskeleton that was a predecessor of myself. The floor was covered with one huge hand-woven rug. Sofas, chairs, and tables were arranged tastefully. Along one wall was a row of screens, which must have been a fairly recent addition. Jethro Hendrickson had used holographic projections. And at the back of this room, before curving windows, was a desk consisting of a large slab of marble on an ironwork pedestal. Behind the desk sat the man I presumed to be Thomas Canard. I advanced to the desk. My escort rushed forward to retain the appearance that they had me under guard.

Canard was surprisingly young. He was a thin fair-haired man of about thirty who had a sardonic twist to his mouth and very direct blue eyes. He stood up and came round his desk to shake my hand.

"Collector, I have heard much about you." His speech was assured and he showed no fear of my hand. He shook it vigorously then gestured to a nearby sofa. "Come, let us sit." We did that thing. "I hear you came to us with one of our people. A woman. Injured I believe."

"Yes, her name is Jethro Susan and she is dying of radiation sickness."

He frowned. "Mmm, unfortunate, but not as unfortunate as might be supposed. If she is the Jethro Susan I think she is then she is wanted for murder."

I nodded and looked back at the guards, damning myself for
forgetting the one the Pykani said she had killed. I changed the
subject while I considered my next move.

"Tell me, why projectile weapons?"

Canard smiled. "Don't be misled. We have not lost the technology. This is merely the result of policy. Interfamily conflicts
were taking a great toll in my father's time and the families came
to an agreement for arms limitations. People are less inclined to
fight when their firepower is so much less. A soldier with an
antiphoton rifle or any other APW thinks he can take on the
world. If he has a machine gun with only a few clips he is more
inclined to discuss matters."

It occurred to me then that this Thomas Canard was a like-
able fellow. I glanced towards the screens and raised an eyebrow.

Canard frowned. "Computing power. More and more processor space is being used for bioresearch projects, and holographic
communication is a luxury." He smiled suddenly. "But of
course you must be aware of how much processor space is taken
up by such research."

I nodded. "I would have thought the thing to do would be to
extend and upgrade your system."

Canard's face lost all expression. "At the present time we are
unable to do that."

Ah, I had found the limit; manufacturing capability; they
were limited to low tech manufacturing and bio' work. I
thought it likely they were not capable of making the required
micro-circuitry, the same kind of circuitry as used in antigravity
control systems, hence the wheeled ground car.

"Oh well," I said, "I guess you can't do everything, but please
excuse my curiosity. You see, I have a request of you and I just
wanted to find out if JMCC still has the back-up technologies
for certain micro-cryogenic operations."

Canard was all smiles again. "What sort of operations would
they be?"

I leant forwards in my chair. "Specifically, the manufacture
of a super-conducting micromesh and bio-gridding of a human
brain."

Canard leant back in his seat, looked up at the ceiling then
across at the guards. After a moment he waved at the guards.
"You may leave." Dutifully and with some relief they headed for
the lift. Canard turned to me again. "Would this concern . . .
yourself?"

I shook my head. "No, I am stable and will be so for a long time yet. It is for another."

He stared at me for a long moment before tipping his head back and speaking at the ceiling. "Computer. JMCC status as to the manufacture of super-conducting micromesh."

The acerbic voice of an old woman I had known nine hundred years ago replied, "At the present time JMCC is unable to manufacture this item. Projections for retooling put capability reclaimable in one hundred and twenty days."

"Computer. Do we have any in stock?"

"There are two thousand square metres of super-conducting micromesh in storage bay one three two."

Canard had difficulty hiding his surprise.

"Computer. How long have we had this?"

"Nine hundred and twenty three years."

Canard sat forwards, his face losing colour, then he shook his head and sat back.

"Computer. JMCC status as to the handling of human brain bio-gridding."

"Capability extant. Present medical facilities have sufficient microsurgical equipment and flash-freeze tooling."

Canard turned to me. "There, it can be done. Now will you tell me who you want it done to?"

"Jethro Susan will die of radiation sickness no matter what treatment is given to her. Before she dies I want her cored and as much of her brain and other nerve tissue as possible to be flash frozen and bio-gridded."

Canard looked perplexed. "Why? All you'll end up with is an organic machine, and not a particularly efficient one. You need the hardware and software to make the grid mutating if you are to give her life. You also need some fantastically complex sub-systems which I don't mind admitting we lost the technology to manufacture ages ago."

"I have all that in hand."

Canard's face went blank for the second time. "Then she will live."

"After the fashion of myself."

Canard stood up and sauntered to a nearby table. From it he picked up an ornate handgun. Salamanders writhed in it.

"I cannot allow that, Collector. I am sorry, but Jethro Susan killed a high status Jethro and must be punished. I also apologise for this," he nodded at the gun, "but I am well aware of your capabilities."

I leant back and spoke at the ceiling. "Molly, cut all the power to the JMCC complex."

"Yes, Collector," came the suddenly eager reply.

The screens went out, then the lights. We were left in twilight tableau. I adjusted my vision accordingly.

"Computer. Restore power to the JMCC complex," said Canard, and I admired him for his calm.

"I am sorry but at the present time I am unable to restore power."

"Computer. Why are you unable to restore power?"

"Cardinal instruction was given to shut down power. I can only restore power by cardinal instruction."

Canard closed his eyes. "We always knew that there was sixty eight percent of the stock unaccounted for." He put the gun down and walked away from the table to another where he picked up a decanter and poured himself a drink.

"Will you do as I request?" I asked.

"Order, you mean."

"If you like."

"Yes, of course I will. We live by certain rules and traditions here and one of those is that what the prime stock holder says, is. Anyway—" he gestured to the marble desk, "you could go and sit behind that at any time you liked."

I said, "It is not my intention to." I looked up at the ceiling. "Molly, restore the power."

The lights and screens came on.

Canard said, "Computer. Convey the general instruction that the Collector's . . . requests have cardinal status."

I stood up. He seemed to be taking this very well. He went on. "We have a very good man in biotech. I'll put him onto the bio-gridding operation immediately. You will want to supervise I presume?"

I shook my head. "I'll be leaving you directly. You have my confidence." Then a thought occurred to me. "You do, of course, have a lot to gain. I will be returning with the requirements for grid mutation and the control sub-systems. The technology will become accessible to you."

Canard smiled. "The thought had never occurred to me."

I saw then why he was chairman. He was sharp.

I walked over to the table and picked up the gun. "Mind if I take this along with me?"

He shrugged. "You hold the controlling interest in it, you might as well retain possession."

I headed for the lift. As it descended I tried not to think too hard about where the piece of technology I had referred to would be coming from.

* * *

Out on the plain night had fallen and the moon with its horns sinister frosted the grass. For a moment I considered what next to do, then I headed for the nearest acacia, collected fallen branches, which I started burning with a quick blast from my newly acquired gun, and sat down to wait. They were not long in coming.

"We have found you, Collector," said Spitfire as she settled on the other side of my fire.

"Yes, you have. Have any mammoth been killed on the plains?"

"Two have been killed."

The rate of kill had increased.

"Point me in the direction of where the last one was killed. It is time for this to be settled."

Hurricane then flapped in to land.

"The Collector is to settle this," Spitfire said to him.

He nodded looked around, then said, "Where is Jethro Susan?"

"She is dying of radiation poisoning in the JMCC complex."

Both Hurricane and Spitfire made a warding gesture.

"We had hoped she might . . ." Spitfire began, then trailed off. She appeared to be very upset. Hurricane had bowed his head and was swaying from side to side. Similar body language to that of a grieving mammoth.

"Where must I go?" I asked.

Spitfire pointed to the south west.

I said, "I will be on my way then. Grieve, but not for too long. I may need your eyes." And with that I set out through the elephant grass. Or perhaps it should be called mammoth grass.

My synthetic skin is as sensitive as living skin, though I have more choice as to what I feel with it—my pain circuits have not been on in centuries. As I walked I felt something on my face, and I reached up to find out what it was. My fingers came away wet. The water I had drunk to supply my sweat glands had supplied my tear-ducts as well.

I set out at a pace that ate up twenty kilometres every hour. Two hours after sunrise I slowed down to allow my joints time to cool, an hour after that I had to stop to take off my boots and remove the synthiflesh covering to my feet. My boots had received quite a hammering from the grass and sandy soil over the last few days and though well made they would not stand much more of this sort of treatment. Ceramal stood up a lot better and my feet could always be replated at JMCC. Good boots had been notoriously difficult to get hold of for a couple of hundred years now and I needed them if I was to keep up a pretence at humanity with anyone I might meet. My trousers were monofilament. I would not know they were wearing out until they collapsed into dust right off my legs.

For the rest of the day I continued at twenty kilometres per hour. That night the Pykani found me and brought more news.

"Another mammoth has been killed near the Kiph. The Kiphani Rainman told us the Silver One was seen in the valley."

It was Spitfire who told me. Hurricane was still at the river Kiph keeping a watch on a family group of mammoth there. I altered my direction according to her instructions and increased my pace. I wanted this finished. As I ran I removed the gun I had from Thomas Canard and checked its charge. It was fully charged, and at full power would be quite sufficient to blow the head off your average cyborg.

The next day the plain began to slope down and develop a few hills. Acacia trees became acacia groves and in places the odd groundsel grew with distorted perseverance. By the afternoon the elephant grass was thinning and becoming scattered with balsams and the occasional patch of bracken. The temperature began to drop slightly and the humidity increase. Then, as if I had run through some kind of barrier I was heading down-slope towards a wall of bamboo. At the wall I halted and removed the panga I had taken from Jethro Susan's pack. Soon I was hacking my way through a twilight thicket. It was damp and miasmic there, and the bamboo crawled with purple slugs.

It was probably the middle of the night by the time I broke out of the thicket and I was not entirely sure of where I was in relation to the river Kiph. I damned myself for only taking the panga from Susan's pack and not filching her compass as well. I might have boosted senses and hyperstrength, but to my eternal embarrassment I could quite easily get lost in a small well-lit room.

Before me was an acclivity overgrown with flowering groundsels and monolithic giant lobelias. I pushed over one of the groundsels, dragged it into a nearby glade, snapped it into metre sections, stacked it, and set it afire with the gun. Then I amused myself as I waited by watching a snail with a shell the size of a human head wearily dragging itself up a branch leaving behind it a trail of eggs like perfect pearls.

Morning was announced by the snarl of some big cat and the humming of sun birds round the lobelias. I had expected the Pykani to see my fire and come, but there was a lot of river valley for them to cover, so I should not have been as disappointed as I was. I threw damp moss over the remains of my fire and headed in the direction I assumed to be west. Soon I found myself in a gorge that eventually opened out into a papyrus swamp, which was difficult going even for me. As the swamp deepened I changed direction again and wondered how long it would be before I ended up going in circles. I had been lost in places of this sort before. Just as I was beginning to regret not waiting at the bamboo grove I caught sight of the river through a hanging mat of vines below which bloomed a fiery swathe of mustard yellow orchids. Eventually the swamp dried up and I was traversing rocky ground on the bank of the Kiph. Luckily, before this sank into swamp again, I saw the canoe.

Her name was Sipana and she was returning to the Kiphani village with a catch of black bass from the river. At first I hailed her from the bank and she drew close to look me over, her unbelievably ancient Optek assault rifle resting across her lap. I thought for a moment she was not going to come to the bank, but she looked at my feet, and to my surprise, smiled and rowed on in.

"You are the Collector," she said cheerfully as I climbed carefully into her canoe.

"That is so," said I, then, "and what are you called?"

"I am Sipana," she replied. "You are lucky. I do not normally come this far to fish." She smiled at me with a perfectly white set of teeth. She was very attractive; wide dark eyes, angular face, topped with coloured beads woven into her dark hair. I looked down at her catch. Each of the bass was a good ten pounds. She had been hand lining for them.

"You don't seem surprised to see me."

"No no, our Rainman said you were coming and to look out for you."

I was surprised. Normally if anyone had word I was heading in their direction they were not there when I arrived. As she rowed us out into the centre of the river I looked down at the bass again.

"You have a good catch here," I said. Something about spending a night and a day pushing through jungle had made me talkative. Human, I guess.

"There are many black bass up here, and trout, we do not fish down stream."

"Why's that?"

"Crocodiles."

I grinned to myself, perhaps somewhat guiltily. I had been responsible for reintroducing the African crocodile into some of the rivers around that area. I changed the subject and our conversation lasted for the rest of the journey.

The Kiphani village was a collection of boxlike wattle huts on stilts on the bank of the river and sometimes straying into the river itself. As Sipana rowed us to a jetty I could see almost immediately that something was wrong. A number of the huts below a huge water oak had been torn apart. As we tied up I could see the look of shock on Sipana's face. I quickly stepped up onto the jetty.

"Any ideas?" I asked.

"It is the Silverman. He was seen . . ."

Silverman? He?

I heard a click as she inserted a clip into her Optek, and I turned round to her.

"Wait here," I said. I removed the pistol from my pocket.

"I have family here," she said.

I looked at her Optek. Responsibility. If the Silver One were to be here and to attack, bullets would do nothing. But what right did I have to prevent her from trying to aid her family? Anyway, I was not so sure the Silver One was responsible. I nodded and we advanced along the jetty.

It soon became apparent, as we mounted the bank, that there were bodies scattered on the ground around the hut. Sipana ran ahead and I did not stop her. There were people walking amongst the bodies, loading them onto stretchers. There was a woman on her knees weeping. Whatever had happened here we had missed it.

As I reached the bodies, five in all, I think; it was difficult to tell. Sipana was standing talking to a Negro nearly seven feet tall, obviously a throw-back to the Masai. He wore decorous green blanket across his shoulders, monofilament trousers, and leant on a gleaming assegai. Across his back was slung an Optek even older than Sipana's. When I approached Sipana tilted her head to look at me and I could see the same Hamitic pride in her features. She waited until I was standing close then looked meaningfully towards the water oak. I looked up and for a moment thought I was looking upon some kind of icon or other object of worship, then I realised. Hurricane had been crucified there.

Anger is a rarity to me. I who over the millennia of my life can be held responsible for the deaths of millions. How many people had been killed by my creations? How many more would be killed? One death should be meaningless. But as always, this was personal. I felt anger then and it was a stark actinic illumination. I advanced to the tree and looked up. Hurricane had been nailed up like the Christos of the Old God, flat broken pieces of metal driven through the bones of his wings and legs, through his body, and into the wood of the tree with great force. He had bled to death. The bark of the tree was red.

"The Silverman came. He nailed up this Pykani and these men tried to prevent him. He tore them like paper dolls. The Rainman would speak with you."

I did not answer him. Instead I removed the covering from my right hand and pulled the spikes from the tree. Hurricane flopped into my arms. I lowered him to the ground; so much flesh. Nothing now.

"One called Spitfire will come. Tell her it is a time for endings. The Silver One will die." I turned from the pathetic corpse and looked at Sipana and the man I guessed to be her brother. "Take me to your Rainman."

They led me to a dark wattle hut, this one cylindrical unlike the rest. Inside an old man lay on a pallet and was being tended to by an old woman in jungle fatigues. The Rainman was black and shrivelled like an old lizard, his hair long and white, and his eyes gleaming. He had been injured. His arm was splinted and his breathing laboured, so I assumed he must have had a few cracked ribs. As I entered the hut he nodded to the woman and she quickly left.

"Welcome to my village, Collector. It is unfortunate that I cannot greet you in the correct manner."

"I have no use for feasting," I said.

He grinned at me. I continued.

"You have something to tell me I presume?"

"The one we call the Silverman spoke to me. The voice was a woman's voice and I wonder if that one is named correctly?"

"Silverwoman should be that particular . . . honorific. I suppose the name changed over the years because she has long not been recognisable as a woman. But it is questionable if gender should be applied to us at all. That is a function of our synthetic covering and of what we were before taking on these ceramal bodies."

"To yourself you are a man. Would you be a woman if you had the appearance of one?"

I warmed to him. He was not stupid. I advanced further into the hut and sat beside him.

"Tell me. Tell me all of it."

"The Pykani Hurricane and Spitfire came to warn of your coming and your purpose. The Silverman . . . Silverwoman is killing the Thunderers and you seek to make her desist. Spitfire flew back to you and Hurricane remained to watch over the mammoth and to look for the Silverwoman."

I nodded. I knew all this. He continued.

"Last night the Silverwoman came into the village dragging Hurricane with her. He was unconscious. She threw him down by the water oak then began to tear our houses apart. I came to her and asked her what she wanted. She screamed her reply, `Tell him to come himself. Tell him not to send his spies. Tell him I'm waiting. Tell him. Tell him.' It was then that Nmoko threw his assegai at her—"

"Nmoko?"

"He is out there. I do not know which one he is."

I had thought for a moment he was the one with Masai ancestry. He must have come later. I could not see him avoiding a fight. The Rainman continued his commentary.

"The Silver One ran to him faster than I could see—" He was obviously uncomfortable with `Silverwoman'—"and tore him in half. Then . . . then others attacked . . . her. They shot her with many bullets, rolled a grenade at her feet . . . Nothing touched her. She killed them. The last of them slowly so others might learn by it. Then she took Nmoko's assegai and broke it into pieces. With the pieces she fixed Hurricane to the water oak. I tried to stop her and she caught hold of me and spoke again; `This is my message to him' she said, and she pointed to Hurricane as he died. `He must come. It's his and his alone. He knows that. I will be at the waterfalls downstream.' We call them the Iron falls, for their colour . . . She then broke my arm and pushed me to the ground."

I nodded and rose to my feet.

"There is something else."

I waited.

"All the time she did not speak she made a sound. It was like grieving and the sounds Hurricane made on the tree . . . Please, Collector, help me to understand."

I considered that. This was something I had not wanted to think about for ages, let alone discuss with a tribal shaman. Yet, it seemed that for each moment since I had climbed down from the ice and the Atlas mountains I had become more human. I held out the claw of my hand for him to see. Hurricane's blood was drying on the ceramal.

"A long time ago I had a wife, and like myself she was made over into metal; given a body to stand against time. Her mind did not. There was too much of the woman and she could not live without flesh. She came to despise me and loathe herself. Until her madness was such that none could draw near her, though she harmed none. Mostly she lived far up on the ice, only venturing down every so often on some aberrant impulse. Now it would seem she has recovered enough sanity to . . . know what she wants. You heard her speak. You are perhaps the first to hear such in five hundred years."

The Rainman looked at me for a long moment and I had to turn away from the compassion of his expression.

"What is her name?" he asked me.

"Diana," I said, and quickly left him, perhaps ashamed there was water enough in me for my tear-ducts, and no urge to cry.

The bodies had been removed from under the water oak and the blood stirred into the dirt. A few villagers were wondering about as if shell-shocked and the sounds of grief could be heard, echoey, from within some of the huts. Sipana and the tall Masai waited. He addressed me as soon as I had climbed down to the ground.

"I would accompany you, Collector, if you will."

I looked at him and wondered if I should allow this. My companions did not seem to do very well.

"What is your name?"

"I am called Kephis. I was not here." Wounded pride and anger warred for predominance in his expression.

I looked to Sipana. "Is he your brother?" She nodded and I turned back to him. The question had merely been a delay while I thought. "Kephis, the Silverwoman—" he looked surprised at the name, "would kill you. Neither assegai nor your rifle would hurt her. She would take you and slowly rip you into pieces so as to anger me. You have a sister and perhaps other family. Stay with them. Save your weapons for the Protestanti, the leopard, and the tyrannosaur, where they will do more than make a few scratches."

"I would come with you," said Kephis.

Sipana looked at her brother in fright. "Kephis, I think—"

"Kephis!"

I looked round. The Rainman stood at the door of his hut. He said, "Five good men have died this day. They fought bravely and well. It rendered them nought. I cannot command you, but for the sake of this village, I ask you to stay."

Kephis looked at the Rainman for a long time, then nodded his head and strode away. Sipana followed him.

"I thank you," I said.

"I would ask you to go in peace," he said. "But I think you would laugh at me."

I laughed anyway and set out for the jetty. I felt guilty about borrowing Sipana's canoe, but I did not suppose she would notice for some time. She had other concerns.

Part Five

I was on the river for an hour with tension making static crackle in my hair, then, just when I was beginning to think I would have an easy ride to the Iron Falls, I saw something long and green with a conspicuous collection of teeth grinning at me from the near bank. He was a monstrous specimen; over ten metres from the tip of his tail to his snout, and no slouch when it came to sliding into the water. I shook my head and looked at the flimsy paddle I held. What had Sipana said? They do not go down river because of the crocodiles. Had I listened, learned, remembered? Of course not, not superior old me. I began to paddle as fast as I could without breaking the paddle.

The crocodile disappeared for a short while then reappeared seven metres behind me, just eyes and nostrils and a huge disturbance in the water. Of course I could have boiled him there with the antiphoton gun. I just did not want to. I suppose, truth to tell, is that I prefer animals to humans. Had an unknown human threatened me I would have killed him without a second thought. I guess it is all to do with knowledge. This crocodile was probably only hungry. Thinking that I looked down at my feet and had an idea.

"Here crocky!"

The first black bass hit the water a few feet in front of his snout. A slight twitch of his head and it was gone. I threw the second one a little behind him and while he turned for it I gained a few yards on him. But in a moment he was back in position. I suppose they were just a taster for him; an appetizer before the main course. He would be disappointed. He would find me easy to swallow—his mouth was big enough—but somewhat difficult to digest. I did not intend to give him the chance to find out. One after the other I threw the last of the bass in a wide pattern, then I paddled like hell as he swirled after them.

The paddle was hitting the water on each side of the canoe like a propeller. I was leaving a mist of water behind me and thought I had a good chance of getting away. Then there was a loud crack and the paddle flew in half in my hands. I caught one half, but the other half landed seven metres behind me, where there was a suspicious looking swirl. The paddle disappeared. Damn! I reached into my pocket and took out the gun. Perhaps I could scare him off. I doubted it.

With leisurely grace he came up beside the canoe as it slowed. He was very close and I got a good long look at his two-metre long head and gently smiling jaws. He was a real monster. I doubted there were any other crocodiles on this stretch of river. This boy would have them for breakfast. The only time I had seen a crocodile of this size before was centuries back and they had been the result of some pretty weird genetic and surgical experiments. I watched him and he just continued to swim along beside the canoe as if grateful of the company. For the life of me I could not understand why he did not attack. One twitch of his head would have this canoe over and in the water. I also found I did not want to do anything about him. A suspicion was dawning; crazy, nonsense. But he was not attacking. He was looking at me with something approaching idle curiosity. His stare did not seem quite as reptilian as it ought to be.

"You're not a normal crocodile are you?" I said.

He blinked. Or was it a wink?

I studied him further and saw that his skull was not right. It seemed misshapen. I tried to remember what those experiments had been. What had been their aim? I remembered. It had been a conservationist group of some kind, from one of the corporate families, trying to make a crocodile with enough intelligence to avoid hunters and to avoid getting into trouble by eating people. There had been some strange ideas knocking about in the corporate families in those days. But that was four centuries ago. Yet, crocodiles could live a very long time, and looking at the jaws, teeth, and size of this one he was a Methuselah. And were they scars round his skull? It occurred to me that their experiments had not been much of a success. This one was not exactly avoiding humans. I leant over the side of the canoe.

"Come closer, Crocky."

Obligingly he drew up close to the canoe. He definitely had scars on his head. I reached down and scratched him behind the eyes with my metal hand and he looked at me as if I had gone a bit far. Then he sank out of sight and was gone.

I waited for a time, expecting the canoe to get bitten in half. It did not happen, so I opened up my pack and got out my sampling kit, then with exceeding care scraped the tissue from the sharp ends of my fingers into a stasis bottle. I had gained something out of this trip after all. With the broken half of my paddle I continued on.

The river wound along its crazy course and I followed it thinking crazy thoughts about sentient crocodiles being more pleasant company than many people I had known. The sun settled above the jungle to be swallowed in mist and the temperature began to drop. I had a fair idea that I would be reaching the falls in darkness, but it was a little while off yet. At the Iron Falls waited my one true love. I could have allowed myself a bitter laugh at that, but I had lost the urge to laugh in any manner back at the Kiphani village. I should have killed her centuries ago as a matter of mercy. Now I was angry and wanted to kill her out of vengeance. But what vengeance would there be if she wanted to die? I wondered about that now. Did she want to die? Or did she simply want to kill me? Perhaps I had got it all wrong. Whether she wanted to die or not was a matter for conjecture. Whether she wanted me to die or not was arguable as well. It was definite she wanted to cause me pain before either happened. Full of bitter thoughts and with my eyes slowly adjusting to the loss of light I paddled on. I was momentarily blinded by the nacreous purple flash that cut the front end off the canoe.

I sat there holding my broken paddle in the sinking canoe trying to put two and two together and coming up with crocodile every time. Then it clicked; antiphoton weapon. I grabbed my pack and hit the water. I sank like a man made of ceramal. Above me, another flash. The canoe was floating cinders, receding.

The river was at least twenty metres deep at that point. I hit the bottom and sank up to my neck in loose silt. Darkness was a cloud of muck. I switched to infrared. That helped me see where the fish were but did not tell me which direction to go. The shots had come from the left bank. Where was the left bank? I decided to walk across the current. Which way was it flowing? I walked anyway, slowed to a caricature of a mime by the silt, bumping into rocks underneath it. This was going to take ages. As a stumbled along I switched from infrared to ultraviolet. That was even worse. I went to normal vision for a while but still could see nothing but clouds of silt. Then I went back to infrared and wished I had not. Being snapped up by a thirty-foot red, green and sapphire blue crocodile is a psychedelic experience.

He hit the silt in a red explosion and his jaws closed on me like two studded doors. I thought then I was about to lose all my synthiflesh, but the jaws halted when they had a grip on me, and he heaved me out of the silt and swam for the surface. Stupid animal was trying to save me, yet he was taking me up into plain view of the marksman, or rather, markswoman. I thought then about what she must want. Did she really want me to kill her? Or did she want to kill me before she did away with herself? Those shots had been close. They could have been fatal. Perhaps she was just not too handy with an antiphoton rifle.

The crocodile brought me to the surface and swam for the bank. I could not see much. I was in white water most of the time. Then we were into papyrus swamp and he was clumping along. Then dry ground below groundsels, on which he dropped me, and stood over me, looking for all the world like a dog that has just retrieved a stick for its owner. I shuffled back from him and stood up to get my bearings. I was on the opposite bank from which the shot had come. I looked at him and shook my head.

"Y'know, I wanted that bank really." I pointed. "Shit!"

His jaws closed on me like a trap. In a moment we were back in the papyrus swamp, white water, then reeds and a steep bank leading up under more groundsels. He dropped me again. Again I shuffled back and stood up.

"Many thanks," I said, stepping out of his reach. "This is exactly where I want to be."

My crocodile saviour gave what I can only describe as a shrug, turned away from me, and with a fair turn of speed headed back down the bank, into the papyrus, and gone. Speculatively I pushed a finger through a hole in my shirt, synthiflesh, and right through to the metal. There were four such across my chest and the fronts of my legs. He had not been so gentle that time. I wondered what he thought I was, and if I had been made of real flesh, how long I would have lasted in his mouth. The temptation might have been too much. I hitched my pack up onto my shoulder and looked around. Now to find the bitch who had vandalized Sipana's canoe. Obligingly there was a flash from down the bank to my right and vegetation turned to an inferno on the opposite bank. I headed for the source.

As before it was difficult going forcing my way through the foliage at the river bank and I wondered what my chances were of coming on Diana unannounced, for I was sure it was she who was shooting at me. It seemed that the fates were with me. Every few minutes or so another shot would light up the banks and I was able to work out my position in relation to her's. At one point, when I was very close to the river climbing over a tangled fall of groundsels, the strike of the invisible beam of antiphotons was directly opposite me and I saw a tree burst into flaming fragments. It was then that I realised she was shooting at any movement on the bank. Her last hit had turned a colobus monkey into a rain of ash. That annoyed me.

Soon I saw I was very close and tried to move more quietly. Then I saw her, only it was not. It was a him. A man in long white robes stood on a rocky promontory poking out from the bank. Immediately I knew what he was. It would seem the Rainman was not the first Diana had spoken to after her centuries long silence. The man standing out there with the APW was what was called a Sheta Protestanti, devil priest in any language. They were the New Fundamentalists or Puritans, worshippers of the Old God before the ice. But they called him the Drowned God; Jesu Christos who had been tied to a chair and drowned for our sins by Jon Batiste. Men not adverse to forcing their beliefs on others by any methods. They considered their ability to cause suffering a mark of their sanctity. It was an old old story. The robes this one wore were called 'pain patterned'. The cloth was stained by being wrapped around the bodies of unbelievers before the poor unfortunates were crushed to death with stones. Around his neck depended a small wooden chair on a string. After a moment's consideration I decided Diana could not have chosen any better allies. They hated me and what I represented, and I would kill any of them without compunction. I picked up a sodden section of tree trunk and moved in.

His concentration on the further bank was such that he did not hear me until I was climbing onto the back of the promontory. He turned, firing as he did so and setting the jungle afire behind me and to my left. I threw the sodden tree trunk at him and it hit him across the chest and arms before the fire reached me. With a gasp he fell back into the river and I quickly dived af-

ter. I caught hold of him at the edge of the rock as he was trying
to crawl out and hoist the APW up before him at the same time.
I picked him up by the scruff, snapped the strap of the APW and
pulled it away from him. He did not seem to be able to use his
arms anyway.

"There's a few things I want to ask you," I said.

All he managed to do was gasp and look at me in confusion. I
dropped him to the ground them sat down nearby while he recovered. It took him quite a while. Eventually he looked up and
spat blood on the rock before me.

"Demon!" he said and looked down, panting, waiting.

"It might well be that I won't kill you," I said, "just answer a
few questions for me and I'll let you go."

"I will tell you nothing."

"Fine, do you think you will still have that attitude after I've
broken a few of your fingers, then your arms . . . oh, sorry, arm. I
see I've already done for the other one."

I stepped forwards. He shuffled back up onto his knees.

"I fear you not, agent of Satan."

"Tell me simply, did the Silver One put you up to this?"

"I will tell you nothing. Do you think I do not know pain?"

"Oh yes, you know how to inflict it. Do you know how to suf-
fer it though?" I reached down and grabbed his broken arm before he could pull away. I twisted it a bit so the rough ends of
bone grated. He screamed with full voice. It should not really
have hurt all that much as he was still in shock and overloaded
with adrenaline. I desisted.

"Now, will you answer my question?"

"Oh God the Father of Christos send to your servant . . ." He
rambled on and on. I could see that if I allowed this to continue
he would work himself into a frenzy and I would get nowhere. I
grabbed him by his broken arm and dragged him to the edge of
the promontory. He yelled, stopped his mumbo jumbo and
hung there sobbing. I took my JMCC handgun out and shot it
into the water. There was a blinding purple flash and a jet of
steam and boiling water five metres high. A lot of it fell on my
captive. He yelled some more.

"Crocky!" I called. "Oh Crocky!"

My friend was not long in coming. Perhaps he had been
hanging around in the hope of more fish. There was a hell of a
swirl then there he was with his nose resting on the rock. He
looked at me with those unsettling eyes of his and as he swished

his tail from side to side to maintain his position it was as if he was wagging it. I wondered just how much Alsatian had gone into his genes.

"You are a demon! You're a demon!" He said it like he believed it this time. He was staring at the crocodile bug-eyed.

"Call me what you like. Your opinions and the opinions of your kind are irrelevant to me. Now, it was a simple question, and she probably wants me to know anyway. Did the Silver One put you up to this?"

There was a long pause, then he nodded his head.

"That's better. She supplied you with the rifle?" He nodded his head again. I wondered where she had cached them and how many more there were. He would not know. "Okay, now, she told the Rainman of the Kiphani she would be awaiting me at the Iron Falls. What else awaits me there?"

"I don't know, demon." It seemed the name had become an honorific.

"Are there more of your kind there, similarly armed?"

He was silent. I dragged him closer to the edge.

"Oh God no! Please, no!"

"Your god isn't here to answer your pleas. There's only one god here and he's a river god and he has teeth over ten centimetres long. Answer my question."

"There are ten!" He said quickly. "Four of them have antilight rifles and the others have flaming swords."

Flaming swords?

"Describe to me these flaming swords."

"Their blades are invisible . . . They only flame when they cut and they will cut a water oak . . . From the handles a shielded wire—"

"Okay, okay, no need to go on. I know what they are."

As he would say; Jesu Christos! Well, it seemed evident Diana wanted me dead and diced. The flaming swords he described were atomic shears with a shear length of up to three metres. I thought back to those cleanly severed tusks on the first dead mammoth I had found. I now knew what she had been killing them with. An atomic shear could cut through anything. It was as simple as that.

"So, awaiting me are five of your fellows thusly armed and the Silver One. Does she have any weapons?"

He looked at me. "She has none. She has need of none. She will bring you down, man-of-metal." Obviously he had regained his confidence.

"It may have escaped your notice but there is a striking similarity between us."

"She does not hold beasts higher than men. She knows God made beasts for men to use in the fields, to hunt for food, to use as they see fit."

"Quite right, I just don't want them to be driven to extinction. Such would be man's loss."

"God would not permit it."

Why the hell had I allowed him to draw me in? I shook him and nodded my head to the crocodile who was still waiting patiently.

"Men are beasts and as a species their future is assured. I think we can afford to lose a few. Would you like to pray?"

"You promised!"

"I'm a demon, remember?"

His scream lasted until he hit the water. He sank then came up quickly, trying to keep his head above water, yelling all the time. Crocky backed off the rock like a submarine pulling out of dock, and sank. The priest was losing his battle to stay afloat when suddenly he shot up into the air in the crocodile's jaws. Those jaws crunched him a couple of times, probably to get the taste, and his yelling ceased. I think it swallowed him under water, because when it came to the rock again to see if I had more fish to throw it looked decidedly smug. There went the other bit about not eating people. I had suspected as much. This was one smart crocodile. He knew which side his bread was buttered on. If that is the correct way of putting it.

I did not feel bad about what I had done. The priest had been a man who had probably tortured many people to death in the name of a god whose doctrines were supposed to be of peace and love, and respect for life. I went out onto the rock, picked up his rifle, and turned away. I felt nothing at all.

Back in the jungle, and I was soon struggling on through darkness with my vision switched to infrared. My crocodile was keeping pace with me, which worried me slightly. I did not want him to get hurt. He could only go as far as the falls though.

All night I pushed on through the jungle. Had I still been in the canoe I would have reached my destination long before. I suspected I would not be there before dawn now. A shame really, as I would have had a definite advantage at night. I could, of course, have waited for the next night, but no, I wanted this over, ended.

I was right. As the mist glowed white and became pink-tinged to the east I heard the low grumbling of the Iron Falls. Soon I found myself cutting through tributaries where the river branched before the drop. The light increased and I moved more warily. At about this time I lost my companion. He had probably gone off in a huff because I had not fed him for a few hours. Soon, after crossing a tributary with a flow which near swept me away, I clambered onto a triangular island of rock abutting the edge of the falls. It seemed a good place to reconnoitre from. Somebody else had thought so too.

It was only luck I saw them before they saw me. Or perhaps it was because I was covered from head to foot in mud. I quickly crouched down behind some heather bushes and watched them from there. There were two of them, changed out of their robes and into dark brown fatigues. One of them had an APW, the other an atomic shear. The one with the shear was speaking into a small chrome egg. I cleaned the mud out of my ears and juiced up my hearing.

"—but brother Jeman has not reported."

The voice which replied was a woman's. I knew it of old. It was the voice of my wife. I was surprised at how much it affected me to hear it again. In my mind she suddenly changed, from a metallic object of vengeance, back into a woman with long dark hair, angular aesthetic features, and hazel eyes that seemed to radiate warmth.

"Brother Jeman was to remain concealed and report his position. It was a mistake to arm him," she said.

"He will be punished, Lady."

Her reply was flat, emotionless. Reality kicked me in the teeth. I realised it had been so before. I just had not wanted to hear.

"I think, perhaps, he has been. Stay alert and continue to report. God be with you," she said.

I tried to shake of the effects of her voice and consider what had been said. So Jeman had kept that from me? Lot of good it had done him. Behind the bushes I unhitched brother Jeman's rifle, knocked down the power and narrowed the beam. Then I stood up, burnt the legs off the one with the shear and the radio, and cut the other one in half. They fell like unstrung puppets.

The one with the radio and minus the legs lay on the ground completely still. The one I had cut in half was making bleating sounds and jerking about all over the place, at least his top half was. I ran over to them, into the smoke and porklike smell of cooked meat. While the halfman managed to get himself tangled up in his own scorched intestines I burnt a hole through his forehead. He was abruptly still. The other one looked at me as if he knew me but could not quite remember my name. I kicked his rifle aside and searched him. He looked down while I was searching and saw what he was lacking. Shortly I had the chrome egg. He looked at me again and there was recognition of who I was and what his situation was. He opened his mouth to scream. I burnt a hole through his palate and put out his brain. There: done. I picked up the shear and dropped it into my trouser pocket, then I kicked the rifle into the river. As I turned to move away from that scene I saw a friend climbing up onto the island and grinning at me. I left him to his lunch and moved to a nearby rock.

"Diana, dearest, oh light of my life."

Her reply was immediate. "You have killed brother Michael and brother Kanga."

"What do you think?"

"I think you are a servant of Satan and will burn in Hell. My only regret is I cannot bring you physical pain to redeem you."

She had found God? I thought it unlikely, more likely she was speaking like this because the others were listening in.

"There isn't that much pain in the world."

"Regrettable."

"Do you want to die my dearest?"

"It is not my destiny to die. I am God's servant and the fulfilment of prophecy. Once you have been sent back to whatever nether hell spawned you I will lead The Brethren against the families and work God's will on this planet."

How did I read that? She was winding me up simultaneous with gulling her other listeners. In a way I envied them their naivety, but, insane or not, I knew I was dealing with a mind over two thousand years old. A mind like my own, mostly. I am not insane of course.

"Do your friends believe all this crap from you then?"

"The truth is here for them to see."

Clever.

"Do they know I was your husband?"

"They know I was in the thrall of Satan and that my years on the ice were punishment for it."

This was getting me nowhere. I sat there for a moment considering and absently listening to the grisly crunching of my friend at his lunch. What now? I had to do what had to be done.

"Tell me where you are then, and we will settle this."

"It is settled already. You are dead."

From a brain netted with superconductor, down nerves of the same substance, the signal was near instantaneous. It took perhaps a few microseconds for the motors in my arm to react. She was slow on the button, or perhaps she hesitated. I like to think it was the latter. The radio left my hand with a sonic crack and was a good fifty metres out over the jungle before it blew. Even so, the flash singed my skin, and the blast knocked me sprawling.

I stayed down as pieces of burning groundsel and heather tree fell about me. I saw a whole tree tumbling end over end into the abyss of the falls. I raised my head higher for a look around. The jungle burnt, then was partially quenched as water rushed back into the blast site. A wave swept past the island carrying blackened detritus and stunned fish. I looked to the crocodile and saw him struggle to his feet, snatch up a pair of gory legs, and with his back smoking, slide into the water and swim away. Typical; you know who your friends are when the going gets rough. I stood up and quickly moved to the water's edge to dunk myself and put out a few of the smouldering bits. As soon as the water touched my shirt it fell to powder. I did not think the guarantee would cover this.

"I'm dead am I? We'll see about that."

I picked up the shear and set out parallel to the edge of the falls. I suspected Diana was below. You could not see the falls from here and she had always liked inspiring scenery.

I crossed three tributaries and a couple of islands before I reached the thick jungle at the side of the falls. A cliff dropped away below me to jungle dimly visible through the mist and spray. Running up from this jungle, keyed into the mossy rock and projecting out to the falls was a spoon fisherman's scaffold. The final platform of it, right at the edge of the water, was empty but for a couple of long handled nets. These the spoon fishermen used to scoop fish from the falls, probably the huge barbel that were sometimes seen in these rivers. I removed my final hand covering, dropped it in my pack, and began to descend.

The rock was damp and slimy where it was exposed and otherwise covered with moss, but the rock face was rugged, with many steps and ledges holding small pools, in which small red frogs and white tadpoles swam, and descent was not difficult. The falls at this point were stepped as well. Soon I reached the scaffold and dropped down onto the projecting platform. From there I had a look around.

From the platform I could see no more than a couple of hundred metres through the spray. The falls were a continuous dull thunder and I could hear little but that. I switched to infrared and picked up nothing but the occasional leap of a barbel as it fought its way up against the water, though for what purpose I have no idea, and the spectral shape of a goliath heron as it strode across the pool below. Where were the spoon fishermen? I wondered, and descended from the scaffold by ladder. Once on the ground I thought for a moment I saw a triangular head poke over the edge far above me. Could have been imagination. I followed a path hacked through the jungle to the scaffold.

The smell of wood smoke gave me fair warning and I was glad my sense of smell was on. It is quite easy to forget things like that. I moved off the path, unhitched the rifle, and continued parallel to it as silently as I could. Soon a clearing and the slow coil of smoke from a fire came into view. I ducked down and crawled the last few metres. There had been fishermen here.

I suppose with what amounted to almost the entire clergy, of this area, of the Church of the Drowned God, all in one place, they had felt compelled to demonstrate their skills to each other. The four spoon fishermen had been available.

I stood up and walked out into the clearing. Three of the fishermen were dead. One of them had been flayed from the ankles to the waist. They had nailed his ankles to a tree to suspend him upside down. All very professional; that way up they fainted less often. Another had been branded and cut with hot knives. His eyes had been put out as well. The third looked as if just about every bone in his body had been methodically broken. The fourth one, who was still alive and groaning horribly, had been suspended over the fire with a rope threaded through the bones of his forearms. His feet were dripping like roast pork. There was a savoury smell in the clearing. With the rifle I burnt a hole through his head and severed the rope. He fell into the fire quite dead. I turned to the other three and burnt holes through their heads, just to be sure. Little else remained for me to do there after that. I followed a path that had been cut through the jungle upslope with atomic shears. It was the way I assumed the remaining Protestanti and my beloved had gone. Emotionlessly I vowed, quite simply, that all of them would die.

By midday I had reached the end of the cut path and come to an area where acacias grew tall and shaded all. The bracken covered ground was fairly boggy so it was quite easy for me to follow their trail. In some places I could see the imprint of my wife's feet and matched it against my own. Slightly smaller, but much the same. I reckoned she must be completely without covering. I thought it unlikely she would bother with it. I sometimes wonder why I did.

The acacias became more sparsely scattered and bracken was displaced by elephant grass. As the temperature rose and the ground became drier I found it increasingly difficult to follow their trail, and I wasted a lot of time following the large tracks of a situtunga antelope, which by rights should have been back in one of the papyrus swamps. Eventually I regained their trail, only now it looked as if their numbers were less. I could not tell if Diana was with them. I considered tracing the trail back to see where they had separated, but decided I had wasted enough time already, and followed the trail before me. This took me out onto savannah, where I lost it at sunset.

When I finally admitted I could see no traces of the tracks of those I was following I spied an acacia tree and set out towards it with the intention of starting a fire. It would draw someone to me; friend or foe. I was fifty metres from the tree when the figure rose out of the elephant grass before me; dark as the night, a foot taller than me, assegai glinting sunset light. He nearly died in that moment. My hand was a claw arcing towards his stomach to eviscerate him before I recognised him. At the last moment I changed it into a fist and pulled the blow. Kephis still oophed loudly and fell to the ground, his assegai stabbing by my feet.

"You cretinous idiot! Never do that to me. You nearly died!"

Clutching at his stomach Kephis rolled his eyes and tried to speak between gasps.

" . . . Collector . . . Spitfire . . . Prot . . ."

I squatted down. "Take your time. You can tell me in a minute."

He took more than a minute to recover and I worried that I might not have pulled the blow enough. It had been a close thing; a split second to damp the motors and snap my hand shut. I could have tried to miss him, but had he moved to one side in that instant he would have been dead. Was I rationalizing? Or had I allowed the blow to land because I was annoyed he had been able to surprise me? He recovered anyway, hoisted himself into a sitting position, and managed to talk.

"I . . . did not know it was you, Collector. I came here in search of Protestanti, like you said."

"How did you know they were here?"

"Protestanti have been in our valley. Four of our fishermen were killed. I come for the vengeance of the Kiphani."

I tried to figure that out. How had he found out? How had he arrived here so soon? I asked him.

"The Pykani Spitfire told us of the fishermen. She was searching for you when she found them. Our village is only four kilometres from here."

So much for my sense of direction. The river must curve back on itself. I should have realised that the Kiphani would not have used the river to get below the falls, what with the crocodiles—Did they know about my big friend?—and the falls themselves to block their way. All they did to get there was make a short overland trek.

"I found your fishermen. The Protestanti are with the Silver One."

"I had no intention of going after that one. I know I have no weapons of any effectiveness. I have come to kill Protestanti."

"Where is Spitfire now?"

"She searches for you still."

I pulled his assegai from the ground and handed it to him. "Well then, you have not changed my plans much. I intended to light a fire to see who would come."

He looked at me dubiously. Lighting campfires at night out on the savannah was something I did and I was unusual in that. People who had blood in their veins did not. The fear was an old one, from when there were GAVs out hunting every night. It was an understandable fear, even now, with only one or two.

He pulled himself to his feet with a grunt and walked beside me to the acacia. There we collected together old wood and a started a fire with a blast of the handgun. He looked at the device with some suspicion.

"The fishermen were killed with such a weapon," he said.

"I killed them."

He nodded his head. "The Protestanti . . . ?"

"Had done their usual work. One of the fishermen was still alive. I am not so sure about the other three. You know what the Protestanti do."

He bowed his head and squatted by the fire. "My sister, Sipana, was much attracted to the fisherman Mkoni. Spitfire told us they had been the toys of Protestanti then killed with energy weapons. I did not like to think what might have happened to them."

"Unless Spitfire tells you, or you look for yourself before the jungle takes them, you will never know. Let it suffice that Protestanti will die for it."

I stirred the fire with a stick before continuing. "You will come with me now, I have no doubt, but leave the Silver One to me. Don't try to kill her. You know you will not be able to. Kill the Protestanti, yes, but even there be careful. They have energy weapons . . ." I trailed off and looked up into the tree hoping to see a familiar dark shape. There was nothing there. Kephis removed a blanket from his pack and sprawled out on the ground. Then with a polite `excuse me', he switched himself off like a light.

Half the night passed. I walked round and round the acacia tree picking up the occasional branch, or bone from the skeleton of a waterbuck, which I stumbled across in the grass, and fed them to the fire. As the dark hours slid by I regretted my lack of humanity. With all I had been through just lately, as a human, I would have been extremely tired, and been able to sleep like Kephis. Of course, had I been human I would have been dead and rotting by now. All I really needed at that moment was a bit of a polish and some repairs of my synthiflesh. Thinking on that I seated myself by the fire and opened my pack in search of my hand and foot coverings, and my boots. All I found was one hand covering and a boot. Somewhere along the line I had lost the rest. After checking I found this was all I had lost. I sighed. This, I suspected, is what you get for indulging in water sports with a thirty foot crocodile. After putting the hand covering on I did another circuit of the tree, picked up the skull of the waterbuck on the way round, and threw it on the fire. Kephis raised his head and looked around, pushed a scattering of embers away from his blanket, then looked at the fire and at me with some annoyance before turning over. It was only a minute or so after when Spitfire flapped to a silent landing on a branch of the tree.

"Welcome, Spitfire," I said, rousing Kephis again.

"Kiphani Kephis has found you, Collector," she lisped at me.

"He has that . . . I am sorry for what happened to Hurricane."

I could not see her face up there on the branch but in her voice I detected surprise.

"You are sorry, Collector? That is . . . gratifying. We should not feel pity though. Hurricane ran out of teeth and is now on the soft flesh of the Grey Thunderer."

Religion was rearing its ugly head all over the place nowadays. I remember when mammoth had only been food to the Pykani. The Grey Thunderer was the great grey mammoth in the sky; clouds, the weather, Earth, God, whatever. And running out of teeth? That is how the mammoth die, mostly.

"I do not feel pity. I just feel angry. The Silver One will die for this as for anything else."

Abruptly Spitfire launched herself from the tree and landed by the fire. I was surprised to see that her eyes were dry.

"For anger or for vengeance's sake kill the two Protestanti to the north of here. Kill them for the mammoth they butchered for a belly full of meat. Hurricane would prefer that."

I stood up. "To the north?" I pointed in what I thought to be the right direction. Spitfire corrected me. "Only two Protestanti, you're sure?" Spitfire nodded. I looked to Kephis. "Shall we go?" After rolling up his blanket he picked up his assegai, hitched on his Optek and pack, stood, and kicked dirt over the burning skull. We went.

The pace I set was much the same as the one I had set for Jethro Susan. In a short time I noticed Kephis was slowing to stay with me. I increased the pace and his run became a yard- eating lope. It was difficult to judge if this was easy or not for him.

"Kephis, you set the pace."

He looked at me, nodded. His yard-eating lope developed a spring that made it look easier and soon I was running at about twenty kilometres an hour to keep up with him. I wondered just how fast he could move if he meant it. I was destined to find out.

Part Six

As the sky slowly grew lighter we saw the topaz gleam of a campfire far ahead of us in a small grove of baobab, acacia trees, and acacia thorn scrub, by scattering of worn boulders. That they had lit a campfire showed the confidence they had in their new weapons; misplaced confidence. At a certain distance from the fire Kephis raised his hand and slowed.

"If we run in from here they will see us," he said.

I had to agree. He had to be a better judge of human vision than me. We dropped to the ground and began to crawl through the elephant grass. It took a long time, but eventually we came up behind acacia thorn scrub and were able to view the figures by the fire.

They were back in their robes now, though they had not abandoned their new weapons. One of them lay asleep with a blanket slung across his legs. The other sat looking into the flames. He had an antiphoton rifle across his legs. He did not look very alert. I turned to Kephis.

"Simple arrangement. You kill the guard when I start running towards them. I want the other one alive."

Kephis nodded and began to unhitch his Optek. I looked at it doubtfully and unhitched my own APW. He shook his head.

"I know this rifle. With that I might kill them both." With a gentle push he clicked the tubular magazine into the Optek, wrapped the strap around his arm and took aim. Then he nodded to me. The next instant I was on my feet and running.

I was through the thorn scrub and halfway to the fire before the guard saw me, and as soon as he did a hole appeared in the centre of his forehead and the back of his head opened like a hairy trapdoor. The sleeping Protestanti jerked awake at the

sound of the shot and looked blearily at the mess spattered
across his blanket, then at his friend who lay on his back in the
dirt, twitching. By the time he got the idea, and was reaching for
his flaming sword, I was on him and hoisting him to his feet.

"Oh God!" he managed as I slapped the shear away.

"No, not really, most of your brothers think I'm a demon, or
the Devil, they can't seem to make up their minds," I said, and
holding him by the back of his neck with my uncovered hand, I
looked around.

From the acacia bushes I had not seen it. I had seen the
wooden spits across the fire, but I had not seen the source of the
meat cooked on them. Standing by the fire now I saw that
source. As Kephis came up I dragged the Protestanti over to the
mammoth.

They had hit the mammoth in the side with the APW, then
moved in and sliced it into pieces with the atomic shear, just as
their adopted mistress had done. Thirty tons of meat, a lake of
guts, hundreds of gallons of liver. As Spitfire had said; they
killed it for a belly full of meat. I did not consider this too
blameworthy. What was the point? As far as I was concerned
they were already under a death sentence. I dragged the
Protestanti back towards the fire while Kephis took a bag from
his backpack. Obviously he hated waste as much as Spitfire, but
for different reasons.

Back by the fire I shoved the Protestanti to the ground. He sat
there and rubbed the back of his neck, surreptitiously eyeing the
APW and shear where they lay.

"Forget it," I said, getting his attention. "You try for them and
I'll break your legs and arms, and we'll still talk."

"You are supposed to be dead," he said.

"An ugly rumour put about by my enemies."

"What do you want?" he asked.

He seemed more reasonable than the last fanatic I had ques-
tioned, he had not called me demon once, so I saw no reason to
go heavy on the threats. I picked up the shear and dropped it in
my pack. I picked up the APW and hitched it over my shoulder
next to the other one I had acquired. I would give it to Kephis,
or perhaps to Spitfire, so she could be like her namesake.

"I want to know where the Silver One has gone."

"I want to live." He looked at me directly. "What are the
chances of that happening?"

"Answer my question and you'll find out."

He snorted. "You have a reputation, Collector, for leaving bodies behind you like footprints in mud."

"If you answer my question I promise I will not kill you." I was thinking Kephis could do the job just as well. "If you do not answer the question I will torture you until you do, then kill you. You have a simple choice to make."

"I might lie."

That was it. I'd had enough. I reached forwards to get hold of his arm and pull him to his feet.

"RUN!!" It was Kephis bellowing as he went past me like a projectile. I looked behind him and saw the reason; a matriarch had found what the Protestanti had done to one of her family group. She was not happy. I ran.

My body is nigh indestructible, but a thirty ton mammoth footpress would do it no good. In a moment I was atop one of the worn boulders and looking down on the scene in the grove. Kephis had made it to one of the baobabs and as I watched he went up it like a gibbon. The matriarch stopped below the tree and looked up at him, showing the whites of her eyes, then she snorted contemptuously and turned away. I realised she must have been with the other when it was killed and have run off. She knew Kephis was not one of the killers, else that baobab would have been flattened, and Kephis with it. I looked to see what had happened to the Protestanti and could see him nowhere. The matriarch had an excellent sense of smell, and on turning immediately charged a patch of thorny scrub, bringing her tusks down in a scoop. There was a castrato yodelling and the Protestanti shot ten metres into the air trailing a length of intestine like a kite string. He hit the ground to one side of the scrub and made feeble scrabbling motions. She was on him in a moment, and she stamped him into a slushy puddle. So much for my saving him for questioning.

Kephis tried to get higher into the baobab when the matriarch came to have another look at him, which was difficult, as it went no higher. Again she snorted and turned away. His crime had not been so heinous as the Protestanti's. She sniffed the air then, but I was not worried. She was too short-sighted to see me, and she would not smell me. After a moment she walked over to the body by the fire and absent-mindedly stepped on it a couple of times. Then she went to the body of the slaughtered mammoth and began to tear up scrub and the occasional tree to throw over it. This was just the start of her grieving. I gave her a decent spell at doing this then I unhitched one of the APWs.

My first shot blew a smoking crater in the ground just behind her. She trumpeted and lumbered round holding an acacia tree above her head. I adjusted the beam width and cut away half of the tree. She dropped the rest and began to charge at the baobab, an easy mistake to make. Quickly I upped the power and beam width and blew a hole in front of her. She stumbled in the smoking crater and backed off. Two more shots and she was on her way to the east, bellowing as she charged off through the elephant grass leaving a cloud of dust behind her.

Kephis took a long time getting to the ground, when he got there I saw why.

"You're shaking, Kephis," I observed

"You play strange games, Collector," he said.

"There was no need to kill her," I said.

He looked towards the retreating figure. "Perhaps not, from where you were standing."

I allowed myself a grin, then I unhitched one of the APWs and handed it to him. "There, you can defend yourself, but please try not to kill any mammoth unnecessarily."

"Unnecessarily, yes . . . "

He took the rifle and slung it over his shoulder.

"What . . . now?" he asked.

"Now I guess we continue to head north. That seems to be the direction they were heading so perhaps the rest went that way. Hopefully tonight Spitfire will turn up and tell us if we are going wrong. Do you still want to come?"

"I must kill the Protestanti who killed my friends, or see them dead."

I nodded. "There are six more of them and the Silver One apparently."

As we started walking he asked, "How do you know this . . . that there are six more of these devils?"

"I had a chat with one of them in the river valley then gave him to the resident crocodile."

"The Old Man?"

I turned and looked at him. "He was an old crocodile."

"That is right and just. I wish we could give them all to him."

"Sipana told me there were crocodiles downstream. She said nothing about this Old Man."

"We do not like to talk of him. He is the spirit of the tribe. He is our icon."

Religion again. I asked no more.

We were walking for perhaps two hours when Kephis pointed out tracks in the dirt. There I saw the birdlike footprint of my wife. We moved with greater alacrity then, jogging along at Kephis's fast pace rather than walking. Following the trail where we could. It went mostly north.

The day dragged on and on and still there was no sign of our quarry. A couple of times I considered abandoning my tall companion, as there was more at stake here than vengeance, but each time I relented. He might come in fairly handy when it came to the crunch. At least that is what I told myself. Sometimes I do not like to look too closely at my motivations. I do not like to be reminded of how human I am.

At midday we stopped and I showed Kephis how to roast the mammoth flesh he had taken with a low setting of his APW. He ate his fill, then paused to drink some water and smoke a foul smelling reefer. When he had finished we moved on and did not stop until darkness. Then we found a suitable tree, built a fire, and I waited while he slept.

Soon Spitfire flapped in to land by the fire. She was about to speak, but I put my finger to my lips and pointed at Kephis, who was snoring gently. I thought it best to let him have his sleep. He'd gone through a trying day. We walked a short distance from the fire.

"The matriarch came," was the first thing Spitfire said.

"Yes, and she nearly did for Kephis. I had to drive her away."

"She knows you were not the killers. She will forgive you."

Anthropomorphism again; a common fault with those who got religion. I wondered where that put me in the Pykani pantheon. I had, after all, resurrected the mammoth. I am legend, soon to be deified. That was all I needed.

"Whatever," I said, "have you any news of the other Protestanti . . . the Silver One?"

Spitfire shook her head slowly. "I have not seen them. Last night I watched the two who are now dead. This night I dare not fly too high. *He* is abroad."

I did not have to ask who *He* was. The GAV was down from the ice again. I think it was more of a tradition than a fear, that they left the night sky to him when he hunted. He had not, as yet, killed any Pykani. Perhaps they wanted to keep it that way. I nodded my head and looked towards Kephis, who was now sitting upright. We began to walk back towards the fire.

"In the morning we'll continue north. It seems the most likely direction," I said, for the benefit of both Spitfire and Kephis. Kephis lay back down. Spitfire squatted by the fire and it almost seemed as if the light of it showed her bones, shadowlike, through her flesh. She looked thin and fey to me. I wondered if the death of Hurricane would be the death of her. I looked thoughtfully to the flames of the fire.

"You say the GAV is in the area?" I asked.

Spitfire nodded. Kephis was abruptly sitting upright again. He was looking up at the night sky dubiously. I went on.

"Then perhaps he will pay us a visit, and we can ask him if he has seen anything," I said.

Without a word Kephis stood up and moved closer to the fire, then he sat cross-legged with his back to it and his APW across his lap. Spitfire looked from him to me then back into the flames of the fire. She did not seem too bothered.

I said, "If he comes, Kephis, do not shoot at him unless he attacks you."

He just nodded.

It was an hour, perhaps more, before I saw in infrared the red bat-shape occlude the stars. He circled us then abruptly dropped for a run. I had seen this sort of thing many years before. I had seen how a GAV could snatch a man from a camp before anyone had time to react. This was why I had considered the Protestanti's confidence in their weapons to be misplaced. Kephis had not seen him, I noticed, but Spitfire had. She hunched lower to the ground and watched him. I stood up and fired into the air with my handgun. The purple flash ignited the night. The GAV broke off his attack run and continued to circle.

"I would speak with you, vampire!" I shouted.

Kephis was on his feet with his APW held ready. He was trying to see what Spitfire and I could see, and failing. I watched as the GAV circled once more then moved in closer. I put my gun away and turned to Kephis.

"Put your rifle on the ground."

He looked for a moment as if he was going to rebel. Then he did as I wished and stood ready to spring in any direction. Only when the vampire landed did he see him clearly, and he nearly stepped back into the fire.

"Machine," said the GAV as he folded closed wings that filled half the night. I noted then he was not so much bigger than Kephis, only a foot or so.

"There's blood on your chin," I observed.

"Holy water," said he, and I suddenly realised he had a sense of humour.

"How many?"

"Two of the white robes."

He turned his head slightly and fixed his febrile ruby eyes on Kephis. Had Kephis not been so black he would have turned white. As it was he took a step back and eyed his APW.

"I would take your head before you reached it, Kiphani."

I said, "There's no need for that. You've fed tonight and these two are under my protection."

His head swivelled again and he seemed to notice Spitfire for the first time. When he spoke again he seemed to be directing his words at her.

"I have mated with human women. My mate has a human man in her nest. She will drink of him when he is done."

I found I was not anxious for Kephis to hear about this. I moved closer to him, ready to stop him if he made a grab for his APW. As I made that move I saw Spitfire was rigid as a statue, her eyes wide open. She seemed mesmerized by the GAV. Abruptly the GAV turned his attention back to me. Spitfire gave a shudder and shook her head.

"You wanted to speak with me, machine. Speak with me."

"The Protestanti you killed. Did they have weapons like ours? Were they with the Silver One?"

"Give me the Pykani and I will tell you."

"She is not mine to give. Why do you want her?" I already had my suspicions.

"Diversity," he replied, and turned his attention back to Spitfire. She began to shiver. My suspicions were proved correct.

He said to her, "Fly with me, little sister."

An unlikely match I thought. He was so big and she was so tiny. There was also the memory of Hurricane to take into account. I was just about to tell the GAV to back off when Spitfire stopped shivering and gave out a strange abandoned laugh. She spoke to him then in a tone of voice that told all she just did not care.

"I will come with you, vampire. I will fly with you. You may love me or kill me . . . Tell the Collector what he wants to know. I will come. Mammoth will be saved and deaths avenged."

The GAV looked at me. "North east of here were six white robes with weapons like that one." He pointed a long clawed finger at Kephis's APW. "I took the two who guarded. Should you leave now you will come on them in darkness. Before I saw them I saw the Silver One walking from the camp. I was curious and asked questions before I killed. I was told she travels quickly to the family complexes. I do not go there."

The family complexes? Did she really intend to lead the Brethren against them as she said? I doubted it. Death. Power. The endless catharsis of hate. They were answer enough.

"I thank you, vampire, and I ask, when you come to the sky, that you do not kill this Pykani."

I put as much threat in the plea as I could. It was wasted. The GAV and Spitfire were staring at each other with heated intensity. Spitfire walked forward to stand at his side. She put her hand on his thigh. The difference in size was even more evident then. But other things were evident as well. She was as small as a child, but sexually she was an adult. The hand she rested on him seemed to be a claim of possession. Chemistry? Madness? Lust? Genetic imperatives? I do not claim to know. I think it was for Spitfire and the GAV to know.

"I will mate with her. As you suggested I will spread my seed and renew the GAVs. Why should I kill a mother?"

With that the two of them launched into the sky.

I was only just quick enough. It was good I had moved closer to him. Kephis had the APW up before him, but his finger had not reached the firing button before I knocked it out of his hands. He swore and struck me across the face. I caught hold of his wrist and the back of his neck and held him while the GAV and Spitfire flew out of sight. He struggled violently at first. When he realised struggle was no use he desisted.

"You told him . . . spread his seed . . . amongst our women?"

I said, "He is partially human and can father children on human or Pykani women."

"Why!? More of them will kill more of us!"

I looked at him. "More of you, you mean. Why should I choose the survival of his kind over the survival of yours?"

"Because you were human!"

It was his best argument. I released him.

"Would you kill all tigers because tigers eat men?"

He looked at his APW and rubbed his wrist before replying. "A tiger does not only eat men."

"Exactly. What do you think a GAV crossed with a man or a Pykani will eat? I think in such a case human flesh and blood will lose some of its exclusivity . . . Are you following me?"

"You tricked him."

"No, I gave him the only course to the survival of his genes he could accept. He will have grandchildren. He may not like them. But he will have them."

He sounded less sure of himself now. "But he is taking and raping women . . ."

"Would you prefer him to go back to the way he was? Better a raped woman than a headless one. Or do you think death preferable? That is often the case with those who don't do the dying."

Slowly he turned and walked to his APW. He looked thoughtful. I expected him to pick it up casually, then as quickly as he could, turn it on me and burn me to slag. He did not. He picked it up and slung it over his shoulder.

"I asked myself about my sister . . . There is a point where pride ceases to be useful . . . We have Protestanti to kill."

He moved to pack his blanket. I eased my grip on the atomic shear in my pocket. A flick of a button and a twitch of my wrist and he would have fallen in half. I was glad he had not tried anything. Wisdom is a survival trait as well.

Two hours of journeying brought us to a place where a pack of hyenas was bickering over the remains of a headless Protestanti; one of the ones the GAV had dropped after feeding on it. Half an hour after that we found the head caught in acacia scrub with its nose gnawed away and a black rat sitting on it like the King of the Hill. Obviously we were heading in the right direction. Half an hour more and we came in sight of the fire. It had been built up very high; an acacia tree had been chopped into logs to feed it. The four remaining Protestanti sat around with their weapons held ready. They'd had a bad night. It was going to get worse.

"How do you want to do this? They're yours," I said.

Kephis tested the weight of his assegai. "I want them away from the fire; in the darkness." He looked at me. "You drive them out into the night, Collector. I will do the rest." And with that he stooped down into the elephant grass and was gone.

I gradually worked my way closer to the fire, close enough to see that all four were armed with APWs. The ones the GAV had grabbed must have dropped their weapons. I imagined that some of this four had atomic shears as well. I set my APW at about medium and aimed at the centre of the fire. My shot ignited the night and I saw embers flying into the air before I got down and crawled away as quick as I could. There were two more flashes and the grass was burning behind me. Another glance showed them on their feet moving away from the fire. I hit it again and watched them diving for cover, shooting wildly in every direction as they went. I got my head down and slowly worked my way forwards. I was about ten metres from the fire when I heard the first scream.

It was the drawn-out and girlish scream of somebody discovering something extremely unpleasant and painful has happened to them. There had been no shots.

"Kenda! Kenda!" someone shouted. There was the crack of an Optek and the horrible smacking sound of a bullet hitting flesh. I heard a rushing sound in the grass. Someone was moaning.

"Christa! Over there!"

Purple flashes brought weird daylight and there was an explosive conflagration. I worked my way in that direction. Hopefully I was behind them now.

As I crawled the moaning became a babbled plea then a scream. Again there was APW fire.

"Chakaree?"

I do not think Chakaree and Kenda were capable of answering. I crawled on, and eventually came across the body of one of them. He had been shot in the arm and then opened from crotch to chest and was trying to say something. Every time he tried he made a sibilant bubbling sound. As I moved past him there was another scream.

"Chakaree? . . . Kenda? . . . Evan?"

I presumed the one calling out the names was Christa. Silence fell. I could hear nothing at the normal level. I juiced up my hearing and listened to Christa's breathing. Even then I could only just hear Kephis crawling through the grass. I waited. Suddenly Christa let out a yell of fright. There was an actinic flash, burning grass, and he was running towards me. I stood up with my APW in my hand, but because of my augmented hearing I had misjudged how close he was. I had assumed he was further away than I discovered him to be. He had his APW in one hand

and something else in his other hand. To my right I saw grass falling as if after the sweep of a very sharp scythe. Something tugged at my right arm and I looked down to see my right hand holding my APW fall to the ground. Then Christa was past me. I swore. Something of moonlight and razored silver flashed past me. It made not a whisper as it hit his back and pierced him. He fell forwards with a metre and a half of assegai protruding from his chest. The point of the assegai stuck in the ground and held him at forty-five degrees for a moment. Then he slithered down it with a choked retching and to lay flat on his face in the grass, bleeding and dying. I turned to the source of the throw and Kephis was before me, starlight glinting off the sweat on his ebony skin. His APW was pointed at me.

"I think that's all of them," I said.

"Yes," said he.

The APW had not wavered one millimetre from the centre of my chest.

"I said I think that's all of them."

"Did you think, Collector, I did not know you had your hand on one of those invisible blades when we talked of vampires and their mating, and of my sister?"

I looked yearningly at my APW on the ground with my hand clutching it like a chrome spider. I had a shear in my right-hand pocket and the handgun in my pack. I could move fast, but not that fast.

"I did think that. Do you intend to kill me?"

"Is `kill' the right word to use?"

"I can die right enough."

Kephis seemed to consider for a moment, then he threw the APW on the ground at my feet. I nearly went for him then, but I showed the most restraint I have shown in many years. I let him live for his temerity. He walked past me and retrieved his assegai from the dying Protestanti, who made a horrible grunting sound when the blade was pulled from him. Kephis cleaned the blade on those pain-patterned robes, and with only his Optek across his back he set out to the south and the Kiphani village. He said nothing more to me.

As I watched Kephis stride off I thought to myself that in a century he would be so much bones and dirt. The thought gave me no satisfaction.

* * *

In the dull light of early morning I wandered to each of the corpses and collected their weapons. Sometime before the light had impinged the sky had clouded over and the temperature dropped. The weather had always been unpredictable this close to the encroaching ice, and I suspected the savannah was in for one of those dramatic winter changes of climate that had, over the centuries, profound effects on the flora and fauna of the area. Changes that had allowed plants like the groundsels to grow on the slopes of the Atlas mountains rather than on the equatorial mountains of Old Kenya as they once had, and changes that had allowed baobabs to grow and were now killing them.

Soon I had collected together four APWs and three atomic shears, and stacked them near the burnt-out fire. If there had been others I did not find them, and hoped no one else would. As I considered how best to disarm them a snow flake spun lazily down from the cold white sky.

Forgetting the weapons for a moment I searched through my pack and took out the few tools I carried, then I inspected the stump of my right wrist and my severed hand. It did not take me long to see that the cut had been through the most complex area of jointing and servo motors of that wrist. I could reattach it, but there was little chance of me getting it working again. I needed high tech tooling; a powder fusion forge for tungsten ceramal, microshear tools, and a supply of servo units and superconductor. There was no way I could do the job properly out here with a few hand-held tools for the working of normal metals. I needed the facilities of JMCC. I put my tools and hand away in my pack, making sure my pack was secure, and turned my attention back to the weapons I had collected.

I could have set one of the APWs to dump its load, but such an act would have been messy, leaving the area radioactive for years to come. There was also the possibility I might need them, or their power packs, some time in the future. Only a few small alterations would make them exchangeable with my own. Instead I turned on one of the APWs and burnt a hole in the ground next to one of the boulders. It took a number of minutes with me standing next a continual incandescent explosion, backing away from the occasional fumarole of slag and molten rock, or fused sand. Soon I had a hole six feet deep. But for one atomic shear and my handgun from JMCC, I dropped the weapons into the hole, then I sheared off a lump of the boulder at such an angle that it fell in and capped it. Perhaps I was being overly cautious, considering that the likes of JMCC could manufacture such weapons at will. But I just did not like the idea of weapons, which could turn me into a deposit of metals on the ground, lying around the savannah like discarded toys. By the time I had finished the snow was coming down more heavily to melt on the still warm ground of the savannah.

As the ground slowly turned wet and muddy I sat on the warm cap rock and considered my next move. I was procrastinating. As soon as I realised this I climbed to my feet and set out towards the complexes of the corporate families. There was really nothing to consider. I had to find my wife, and kill her. For the sake of the mammoth, the Pykani, and the Kiphani, she had to die. But most especially for the sake of Jethro Susan. And for her my wife had to die in a very special way.

The snow continued to fall and the cold to work its will on the land. By midmorning there was a layer a centimetre deep and small icicles were appearing on the odd acacia I passed. With this drop in temperature I upped my pace to twice what it had been with Kephis. That I had not done this on leaving the Protestanti's camp was indicative of my reluctance to face Diana. A voice on the radio was one thing, as were second-hand reports of the Silver One, but to come face to face with her and kill her . . . that was another thing entirely. By midafternoon I saw the first blurred birdlike footprint in the snow and knew I was not far behind her. I increased my pace.

As the afternoon drew on the footprints did not get any clearer. This was either because she was moving at a pace comparable to my own or because the snow was coming down heavier now. A layer of it covered the front of my body as I ran. Every so often I had to stop and knock away where it had been frozen into a thick crust by the wind chill of my passage. Again I increased my pace. The snow was now a good three inches deep and beginning to drift. This put more strain on my motors and my joints began to heat. Soon the snow ceased to settle on me.

As the afternoon drew to a close her tracks became clearer. In the evening, when the light began to bleed away, I switched to infrared, but there was nothing to see. I realised that even though I was so close I could lose the trail. I tried ultraviolet and saw her footprints glowing like neon signs. Of course, she could not have been much further away than Jethro Susan and myself when that APW dumped its load. She was radioactive. I looked behind and noted how my footprints glowed just as much.

Into the night my run continued; as lurid as in any computer game. I wondered when it would end. It occurred to me then she might be heading back up to the ice. Perhaps her madness had returned. Then, like a dire wolf in the night, a howl.

Diana.

She should have died like a human after a small span of life. Her immortality should have been the old genetic immortality of children. I should have killed her long ago and saved her the pain that made her howl like that.

After the howl came an echoey sobbing as of someone lost in a cavern. She shouted a name then. And it was mine.

Did she regret or did she name me in hate?

I saw the burning shape ahead of me, standing, then falling to its knees in the snow. I slowed as I pulled the atomic shear from my pocket. I should not have slowed. I should not have hesitated. For she said my name again and the tone of her voice left a seed of pain in me. As I closed in she said no more. The atomic shear bucked in my hand as I swept it across. Her head thudded into the snow like a rock. Her body swayed with electric sparkles flashing round the stump of her neck, and fell shortly after.

* * *

As if the storm had been only for us the sun rose over a flat white landscape with an excess of light. Snow crystals glittered like a sprinkling of silver dust and a nearby acacia looked like a sculpture of glass and white cotton, scattering rainbows all around. I had not moved for a couple of hours nor had I looked at the headless metal body beside me. Motionless I had knelt there trying to feel something; anger, grief, satisfaction. All that happened though was that I found my mind wandering. I thought instead about crossbred vampires and humans, sentient crocodiles . . . Mostly I came back on what I had to do next. Slowly I turned and viewed what remained of my wife.

The body beside me was like a skeleton over which had been stretched a thin film of silver. Her spine below the squarish ribcage was a three-inch wide column and the metal of her legs and arms was thicker than bone. The main difference between her and the inner me was the shape of her ceramal pelvis. It was wider, with the tops of her legs sloping inward so that when she was covered with synthiflesh she had the hips of a woman. But she had been without sythiflesh for a long time now. The metal of her feet and hands was worn to the extent that the knurling was gone. I noticed she was missing a couple of toes and fingers as well. I turned away and looked for her head.

It had sunk in the snow; a shiny ceramal skull with white enamelled teeth and eyes like mirrored spheres. Her storm shutters had come down at the last moment. I felt the ridiculous impulse to say something beginning with `Alas . . .', but the impulse went when the storm shutters rose and I was looking into her grey synthetic eyes.

I nearly dropped the skull. All those hours I had sat there thinking it was over. Idiot! Like myself she had a small secondary power supply set in the base of her skull. Separating her brain from her main power supply had not been enough, just as breaking through the insulation of her flash frozen nerve tissue had not been enough. The cold, perhaps had slowed things, as had the integrity of the superconductor grid in her brain. She had no need of oxygen or blood, just cold and power. She was still alive. I turned the skull away from myself and felt its jaw move. I tried to tell myself she was not screaming. I searched in the snow for the atomic shear, found it, and sliced a scale of ceramal from the base of her skull. Inside was a small area densely packed with microcircuitry divided from her brain by a transparent film. I located the thumb-sized power supply and pulled it out. Blue sparks showered the snow. When I turned her back to face me the jaw stopped moving and the storm shutters were back down. I sighed. For an indefatigable cyborg I felt incredibly tired.

Again I sat there for a while. Inertia seemed to be my greatest problem now. It took a severe effort of will to remove my pack and drop the head inside. Then I climbed to my feet like a creaky old man, put my pack on again and stooped to the body of my wife. She was heavy, three times the weight of a normal woman, and as I set off across the whiteness my feet sank deep into the snow and the damp soil below.

* * *

On the evening of the second day I reached the JMCC complex. The snow had melted and for most of that day I had been stomping through slushy mud and a steamy mist. The groundcar came out when I was the same distance from the complex as when last I had come here. I wondered, irrelevantly, if they would get tired of me bringing bodies in.

"Collector," said the guard captain as he climbed down from the car. He was the same one as before. I nodded to him and he watched as I slung Diana's loosely articulated body off my shoulder and dropped it with a crash in the doorway of the car. I climbed up and hauled her inside. He looked at the dents and scratches I left and attempted to conceal his chagrin. I apologised absently and he looked at me in amazement before following me inside. But for the three of us there was no-one else in the car. The guard captain sat in the driver's chair without a word. Soon we were speeding back to the JMCC. Only as we reached the hangar doors did he finally get up the nerve to say something.

"You lost your hand," he said.

"Temporarily."

"We were told you have cardinal status."

"Yes, I do."

That was all he said, not a word about the headless ceramal body on the floor, not a complaint about the stink of decaying flesh from it and from my pack.

In the hangar I stepped from the car to be greeted by Thomas Canard. He was as well dressed and suave as before. I looked like somebody's nightmare. I probably was at times.

"Welcome back, Collector."

He looked in the door of the car then gestured to a number of personnel who had foolishly been standing by looking as if they had nothing to do.

"Take that to Jenson in Cryo."

I held up my only hand. "Wait a minute." I unhitched my pack and removed the metal skull. Putrid brown fluid ran out of it. "This goes with it."

A woman in coverall and with black hair, cropped like Jethro Susan's had been, took the head with her face twisted up in disgust. I saw her grab up a piece of plastic to wrap it in as soon as she could. It took four men to carry the body away.

"It won't be too damaged, will it?" asked Canard.

I shook my head. "It was a clean cut at the neck with an atomic shear. Once the old tissue is removed it'll be usable. The head is only a fancy case. The important subsystems and their software are in the main body, still under power."

He nodded. "There should be no problem. I'd suggest you go with it to have your hand seen to, but I suppose you want to speak to her first."

"Speak . . . ?"

"We are not completely primitive. We were able to give her voice and a little usable memory."

I was surprised and gratified. If they were able to do that then they were much less likely to louse up the main operation. Canard led me from the hangar, through corridors and rooms where technicians ran about in frenetic contrast to what lay outside the complex, to a white walled room with a single chair at its centre.

"I'll leave you with her," said Canard, and closed the door on his way out.

I looked around the room. The only sign of instrumentation was the snub nose of some kind of projector up in one corner. I sat down in the seat. I felt I needed to be sitting, why, I do not know. I had expected to see a cryonic tank in here at least. She was somewhere else then. As I sat down the air before me flickered. And she was there.

"Collector . . . "

"Hello, Jethro Susan."

"How long . . . ?"

"Days only."

"You . . . I . . . was dying. Why have you done this to me?"

"It seemed just."

"You are punishing me?"

"What have they told you?"

"There . . . were tests . . . They told me what I am. I have been gridded. My mind is held in stasis like your own. Only my mind cannot change with time. I have a small memory, but it is a computer memory."

"My mind is enabled to grow and to alter like a living mind with the aid of complex software and even more complex hardware installed in line with the grid. JMCC did not have this technology. I got it for you."

"You . . . killed the Silver One."

"And I brought back her body so it might be yours. Subsystems included. You can live again."

"I will be like you."

I could not think how best to reply to that. Would she be another one like Diana? Driven mad by the lack of flesh?

I said, "Your inner structure will be of ceramal. Outside you will have synthetic flesh with all the advantages of human flesh and few of the disadvantages. You will be human. And you will never grow old and die."

Silence met my words. I thought then about Diana and what had probably driven her over the edge in the end. She had lost her synthetic covering and with it the last vestiges of humanity. Ceramal does not feel. For us it is the weak outer covering that is our shell. The weak outer covering that keeps us human.

"Jethro Susan . . . Susan . . ."

There was no reply. Shortly the door behind me opened and Canard walked in.

"My cryonic man, Jenson, tells me he just took her off line to prepare her for installation. Sorry about that. Now, your hand."

He led me to a place where a technician reattached my hand with a relish and enthusiasm I found disquieting, then to another place where a similar technician provided me with synthiflesh covering for my hands and feet.

"You see? Linked into your system they give more sensitivity than your others. Do you agree? We use a new neural fibre satellite-grown for . . ."

He rambled on and I nodded my head in agreement with him. He was right. My hands and feet were more sensitive. But I was still worrying about Jethro Susan. Was I doing the right thing? Or was I making another Diana? I remembered competitiveness when we hacked our way through jungle with her panga. But I also remembered her reaction to me when I pulled my face off in Z'gora. There was that time with the vampire as well. Did she remember it all? Or did she think it a nightmare? Abruptly I realised what my speculations were. I was not worrying about her sanity. Like a teenager on his first date I was wondering if she would like me.

I nodded my head, smiled, and gritted my teeth with self-contempt as the synthiflesh technician turned his monologue to synthetic sexuality.

A night passed, another day, another night. I fretted like the husband of an expectant mother. On the day things were coming to completion, Jenson, the cryonics man, lost his temper and swore at me, then turned white when he realised what he had done.

"I'll leave you to it," I said, and left him to it, which no doubt surprised and pleased him. I went then to bother the synthiflesh technician, who had now turned to making the outer Jethro Susan. He was much more amenable but harder to get along with. Some of his questions were personal to the point of obscenity. I left him, and after a great deal of trouble got someone to make me a pair of boots like my old pair. Then I went outside.

The sun was shining, but there was a chill in the air, which I especially noticed on my hands. I sat on the fallen trunk of a baobab and watched a large family group of wild dogs yipping and bickering their way across the savannah.

"Hold it right there, you bastard!"

I spun round, slipped, and tried to catch hold of a branch. The branch snapped and I fell backwards off the log to land with a heavy thump.

When I came up spitting leaves from my mouth I said, "I suppose you've been waiting for that for a long time?"

Jethro Susan's laughter was music.

THE ARMY OF GOD
AND THE SAURAMAN

I was twenty metres up in the branches of a prairie elm—a splicing of elm, redwood, and stinging nettle—and so intent on collecting the microscopic seeds of the orchid that I didn't notice the men until they were below me. As soon as I heard the voices I looked down and instantly became curious: I did not recognise the uniform, though it had parallels in the far distant past, and as far as I knew no-one on Earth had been taking slaves for at least a hundred years.

There were four men dressed in black, with skirted helmets of mirror metal on their heads, and rapid-fire projectile weapons in their hands. They were guarding a neck-yoked and manacled party of about twenty ragged men and women. These people were loaded down with equipment that I focused in on and identified as a variety of fuel-driven cutting implements. I watched them pass under the tree then after securing my sampling pack to a branch, I scrambled to the ground and followed.

The buzz of the chain saws located the group for me when for a short time I lost sight of them, and if that had not been enough the fall of a hundred foot elm would have been. I sneaked in close and watched them from a ridge tangled with lianas and infested with poisonous spiders the size of apples. The creatures were tenacious, but after testing their fangs on my skin a few times they soon lost interest.

The slaves, now freed from their yokes but still manacled, were stripping the branches from the elm and cutting away the top shattered section. The guards had seated themselves at a vantage and were smoking something which, by the giggles, I figured was not tobacco. I settled down to watch, only mildly annoyed at the destruction of this fine tree. The loss of one or two of them would be no problem, but if these people went into wholesale lumber-jacking I knew I would have to do something. The tree orchid had only just managed to get a foothold here.

In the hour that followed they cut the tree into thirty-foot sections then split it into rough planks as thick as a man's body. When these were stacked, one of the slaves approached the guardsmen. Something was said, perhaps about the work being completed, and one of the guardsmen rose and followed the slave back to the tree. When he got there he walked to one of the slaves who was lying on the ground, stood over him, and began shouting. This second slave slowly dragged himself upright and as he did so I noticed the other guardsmen had risen and were approaching also. When I turned my attention back to the first guard I saw him strike the slave in the belly with his weapon. I don't know what came over me then. I should not have interfered. I rose from my bed of spiders and began walking down the slope. The guards saw me immediately, and grouped together to watch me approach. Their stance was hesitant at first, then after something was said, casually arrogant.

"Good morning," I said.

A guard with burnt-black skin and a ginger goatee, grinned with wide white teeth and turned to one of his companions. This one was a short bow-legged bushman.

"The Lord Provides," he said.

The bushman looked at me warily then pointed his weapon at me. I did not consider this a civil greeting and considered killing him, but my curiosity was roused, and dead men don't answer questions.

"There's no need for that," I said mildly.

"You are correct," said ginger beard. "You have come here unarmed to offer your services to the Drowned God. Why should we threaten you?" As he said this his companions moved forwards and ranged themselves about me. I kept a wary eye on the bushman as he moved close in to my left.

"Drowned god?" I wondered.

"You are unenlightened," said ginger beard. "Enlighten him, Chakra."

The rifle butt struck me in the base of the spine and bounced. Chakra swore as I turned towards him. He hurriedly stepped back. I snatched his rifle from his hands before he could get too far and snapped it in half, then I turned back to ginger beard. He now had his weapon pointed at me, as did the rest of them. Some new religious cult, I surmised. There seemed little more worth learning. I regretted the impulse that had brought me to this confrontation, and I was annoyed by the predictable behaviour of these men.

"Who are you?" asked ginger beard.

"I am sometimes referred to as the Collector. Now, I merely came down here to ask who you are and how many of these trees you intend to take down."

"We will take as many as the Bishop requires."

I noticed that the bushman's face had taken on an unhealthy pallor, as had the face of the one white-skinned guard. They, I assumed, were the only two that knew of me.

"Sir," said the whitey. "It would be best not to take this any further."

"Yes, you are perhaps right," said ginger beard, and put three rapid-fire shots into my chest.

I staggered back and swore. Now I was really annoyed. There had been no need for that. As I regained my balance I saw the bushman sprinting away just as fast as he could and whitey backing away nervously. I stepped forward as ginger beard fired again, took his rifle off him and swung it in a short arc ending at his companion's head. With a crunch that one's head deformed and he dropped to the ground. Before ginger beard could react, I took hold of the front of his uniform, lifted him off the ground, and looked round at whitey. He turned and ran.

"Now," I said. "I would like some answers. What is this wood for? And where is it to be taken?"

He made some gagging sounds so I lowered him to the ground so he could reply.

"The wood . . . is for the Cathedral to the Greater God. It goes south . . . south into Cuberland."

"I see, now, your uniform. I do not recognise it."

"We are soldiers in the Army of God," he replied, as if this was meant to impress me.

"How many trees do you intend to cut down in this region?"

"The cathedral is a great work!"

"How many trees?"

"I don't know."

"How large is this army of god?"

He did not seem inclined to reply to this question so I reached out with my other hand and snapped his wrist. After he'd stopped yelling, he became a little more co-operative.

"We are . . . five thousand."

"And presumably there is a priesthood as well?"

"Yes . . . I do not know how many . . . Please! I don't know."

That seemed about as much as I needed to know so I then checked through his pockets until I found a set of rough-cast keys. These I tossed to the slave who had not yet dared to rise from the ground. He grinned at me viciously, selected a key, then unlocked his manacles. As soon as he had done this he tossed the keys to another of the slaves and rushed to pick up one of the weapons.

"What are you doing? They are the property of the Drowned God!"

I considered killing him then and there, but after looking round at the gathering slaves I realised that here were people more eager for the job. I threw him down in the dirt and wandered over to have a look in the packs the guards had left at their vantage.

The first two packs I opened contained nothing but food and spare ammunition. The third pack I opened contained a much thumbed book written in Urtak Swahili. From this I discovered the doctrine of the Drowned God and found it little different from all the forms of fundamentalism I had encountered down the years. The whole mess was a weird distortion of Christianity. Their god was called Jesu Christos. There was no trinity. Their main icon was the chair he was drowned in by John Batiste. He died for our sins apparently. I thought him a bit premature. As I speed read this book I kept an eye on the slaves and saw that out of one of the planks they had made a pole with a suspicious looking spike carved on the end. This they had set in the ground and were meticulously sanding and removing the tip of the point from. Ginger beard was lying on the ground tied to a plank and weeping. I opened the last pack to see what else I could find.

The last pack contained all sorts of strange paperwork. There was a list of punishments for crimes ranging from heresy to petty theft. The cult of the Drowned God was very big on severe punishment. It looked to me as if ginger beard was about to get number twenty-four on the list; the punishment for assaulting a soldier of the army of God. I watched them as they greased the

end of the spike with lubricant removed from the cutting implements. As they started to strip-off ginger beard's clothes I wandered over and methodically smashed the saws. These at least
would not be used to cut down any more trees. The chief slave
approached me when I had finished.

"Collector, we thank you," he said with a bow.

"Think nothing of it," I said as ginger beard was carried
screaming to the spike with ropes tied to his ankles. "Why did
you blunt it?" I asked.

"A sharp spike will penetrate vital organs and he would die
too quickly. This way it will take him days."

"I see," I said as I went to collect my specimen pack. Behind
me the screams reached a crescendo then became interspersed
with agonised groans. I felt nothing.

My next encounter with those who styled themselves The
Army Of God was not long after my first and not wholly unex-
pected. I had remained in and about the forest of elms to await
developments. I had no doubt that a report of my actions would
reach the Clergy, though not necessarily from the escaped soldiers; such men might not consider it politic to be the bringers
of such bad news, it might be unhealthy for them.

This time it was no guard detail leading slaves that came to
the forest but a disciplined military unit of twenty-five men and
women. I watched their cautious approach from deep in the forest, hidden in the shade of dark-green cycads. I considered coming out to face them but numbering their weapons I decided
against this. Hits from such weapons would be unlikely to kill
me, but the bullets could entirely strip my outer covering and I
would then have a long trek to one of the complexes to get another. It was fear of inconvenience rather than fear of death that
caused me to stay hidden.

After removing their comrade from his stake—I believe he
had finally died sometime the night before their arrival—the
unit methodically searched the area. This they did for three days
before setting up permanent camp on the edge of the forest. I
watched as radio messages were passed, then watched again as on
the morning of the third day another guard detail came into the
area with a couple of hundred slaves. Many of the slaves carried
nice gleaming chain saws with ceramal teeth and compact
power-dyn engines. I reckoned these had come from one of the
corporate families and felt a hint of unease. What, I wondered,

had been bartered in exchange for these tools? Most Earth-bound organisations had no currency to interest those hugely wealthy satellite-based families. It was perplexing, and whereas I had been about to intervene and ask about the cutting of trees, I held back. This was fortunate. Over the next two days I came to notice that though most of the soldiers carried rapid-fire opteks, there were others amongst them who carried weapons I at first could not identify. I was wondering if perhaps some group, separate from the families, had reinvented the QC laser, when my wonderings were answered.

Though worn to the bone by their treatment there was still spirit in some of the slaves. I recognised some of them by tribal marking and physical irregularities. There were proud people here only awaiting their chance. It was in the night that some of them took that chance.

Being very much a spectator in all things, I had flicked my vision over to infrared, and secured myself in the top of an elm to watch for the night. The moon, with its face ordered and cut like an integrated circuit, was full, but more often than not clouds obscured its light. I suppose it had not occurred to the guards that it wasn't a good idea to provide the slaves with tools that could cut through their forged iron chains as easily as they cut the wood of the trees. A chain saw started in the middle of the night and of a sudden there was chaos down below. Slaves were bolting into the forest and guards were running back and forth and shouting. Then there was a stuttering purple flash and I saw a man momentarily silhouetted before he disintegrated. Abruptly I felt quite vulnerable up in my tree. Someone had provided these people with weapons that could kill me. I was less than amused as I descended from the tree and crept into the shadows, and more than a little confused: like the chainsaws, such weapons had to come from one of the corporate families. Perhaps one of them had some sort of agenda beyond sacred profit.

Stalking away from the camp in the darkness I extended the range and depth of my hearing, as well as my sight, as a precaution. I heard him before I saw him. It was the severed metre of chain he held in his right hand that I heard clinking in the night. He was one of the slaves who had escaped. This much was obvious. One of the 'Army of God' would not have been slinking in the bushes like this. He was almost certainly going to attack me.

It is a fact, unfortunate to many, that I do not hold human life in high regard. Let's face it; evolution has provided human beings with a more than adequate facility for survival. This is why the culling of the human race had become a necessity within the history of my span; why the Great African Vampires had been engineered to feed on human beings, and why human beings had been engineered into the vampiric Pykani so they could feed on easily renewable resources like mammoth blood. The cull had saved us as a race by freeing sufficient resources to enable us to get into space and find lebensraum there. Us . . . how readily I use that word: I who ceased to be human a thousand years ago.

It is also a fact that I am called The Collector for a very good reason; I am a collector and curator of the genetic heritage of Earth. I value this diversity more than anything else, because once lost such complexity is lost for ever. It can be replaced. There are technologies in existence for the creation of complex life. Without its genetic information, a buttercup can still be recreated from pictures, but it won't be a buttercup. Picky, but that's me I guess. It is that side of my nature that saved my attacker's life.

The man was naked, squat, and heavily muscled. He was light-skinned and had curious diamond-pattern markings extending up his back and over the top of his head. He swung his length of chain at me very hard and, as I later discovered, had I been truly human it would have literally taken my head off. I caught this chain and drew him towards me—he was still manacled at the other end—with the intention of breaking his neck. It was when I saw that the markings were in fact scales that I let him live. Here was something I had heard about and dismissed as the workings of fabulists. Here was a sauraman; a splicing of human DNA and DNA built from imprints on fossilised bones.

"Desist, I'm not your enemy," I said.

The man continued to struggle against me even though he could not escape from the hand I had round his neck. I considered rendering him unconscious, but had no idea of the strength of his skull. It is true that, had I killed him, I would still have had access to his DNA, but I was curious. And when you have lived for as long as me, something of interest can be a life saver; ennui being the greatest killer of my kind.

I tripped him and sat him on the ground. He kept fighting me even from there, hooking blows at me, with his left hand, that would have caved in the ribs of a normal human. As he fought me I saw that his eyes had slotted pupils that were dilated; he could see in the dark. I threw him to his back and pinned him with my knee. Releasing his throat I reached round and caught his left wrist. Still he fought, attempting to throw me off. I noted a degree of surprise in his expression when he discovered that he could not lift me. Yet, he simply would not give up. I was beginning to get a little irked and considered taking the risk of knocking him unconscious when I heard the soldiers approaching through the forest behind. I tilted my head to the sound and abruptly the sauraman was still underneath me. His hearing had to be superb if he heard them as well.

"These are the enemy," I said.

The sauraman just lay there and stared at nothing. Damn, I'd killed him, I thought. I was about to release him when I realised he was playing dead as do some of the snakes to which he was distantly related. I also wondered if he understood my words. Perhaps he did not. Perhaps he thought I was with the soldiers and playing possum like this, now he knew my strength, was the only way he could escape. I had to show him that I was on his side. I could kill to do this, but this would put me in danger of losing him should he run or losing him should he join in with the slaughter. I took another option.

I listened until the soldiers were close, to be sure that even a man with less than average hearing would hear them. They were still a way off, but they made no effort at silence or concealment these soldiers of God. Abruptly, as if I had only just heard them, I released my holds on the sauraman and leapt up. I then fled into the forest. What happened next I should, in retrospect, have expected. Here was a man who had been caught, enslaved, and brutalised by this 'Army of God'. Here also was a man who could see in the dark, was perhaps three times stronger than a normal man, and was, to put it bluntly, a predator. I had been a surprise to him. He had perhaps thought me some kind of forest demon. His tormentors he knew and he had them right where he wanted them.

I had gone perhaps a hundred metres before I realised he had not fled with me. I stopped and listened and realised that he was

circling back. He was good, very good. I had to have my hearing
at its optimum to catch him sneaking back upon the soldiers. I
crept back after him, worried for his safety. I need not have worried.

There were five soldiers. Four of them were armed with
opteks and one carried an APW. This I discerned after climbing
an elm to get above the undergrowth for a better view. They were
walking through the darkness with torches, talking, and smoking cannabis cigarettes. The sauraman was lurking in the undergrowth five metres ahead of them. He had not been evading cap-
ture when I had come upon him, but lying in wait. He came at
them from the side, his chain swinging in a tight vicious arc. I
saw one soldier standing for a moment minus his head and another going over with the side of his head caved in. The former
had been the one with the APW. A torch bounced off a tree and
lay flickering on the ground. My sauraman went into the next
soldier and drove his hand into his guts. There was a high
pitched scream and he was discarding a handful of intestines.
An optek stuttered in the darkness, but I did not see it fired as by
then I was down my tree and moving in.

A soldier came running towards me through the dark, firing
at the bushes and the trees. I stepped behind one of the trees,
waited until he was opposite me then reached out and chopped
him across the back of his neck. As he went down, I heard the
last soldier yodelling in agony. Then there was silence. I walked
towards that last scream and the sauraman came from it to me.
In the darkness we stood about five metres apart and looked at
each other. The sauraman now held an optek that he pointed at
me. I expected him to use it and that finally I would have to kill
him. He did not. He grunted and went back to the four dead soldiers. I followed.

"You understand now that I am not your enemy?" I asked.

The sauraman ignored me while he raided the dead. For my
own peace-of-mind I went and took up the APW and its spare
power packs. He looked at me for a moment then continued
with what he was doing. He stripped the least bloody of the
corpses and fashioned his jacket into a loin cloth held with a
belt. The clothing would not have fitted his squat and muscular
frame any other way. Two of the soldiers had rucksacks into
which he put spare ammunition, money, knives; anything of
value or utility. He was very thorough. The opteks he tied together with the pair of trousers. He made a carry strap from an-

other belt. I looked at his haul and thought he would certainly have trouble carrying it all until he it became evident, when he dumped the two rucksacks in front of me, that he did not expect to. I obliged him by picking them up. Into one of them went the spare power packs. He then demonstrated that he could have carried it all, for he took up the roll of opteks, belts with holstered pistols and other items such as water bottles and the like, on one shoulder. Over his other shoulder he slung the stripped corpse, before setting out at a jog into the forest. I followed, content at the moment to just go with the flow. He interested me.

That night I suppose we travelled ten kilometres into the forest. My companion, with unerring senses, found a place where trees had fallen to provide a cosy shelter. He dumped the corpse outside and his loot inside. I put the two rucksacks inside as well. From the APW I removed the power pack before putting it inside. Once this was done he built a fire and ignited it with one of the lighters taken from one of the soldiers. I squatted at the other side of the fire while he went about this, and in the dull twilight I studied him more closely.

His hands were thick-fingered, and rather than fingernails he had hard curved claws as blunt as a dog's. He was completely hairless and completely scaled. Those scales on his head and down his back were the largest and most evident, being thumbnail sized. The rest of his body was covered with scales only a couple of millimetres across. Halfway up his forearms and up the back of his calves he had spur claws. His eyes, as I have mentioned, had slotted pupils. They were the eyes of a snake. His ears were pointed, and I have to wonder if that feature was a conceit of the geneticist who had spliced his kind. His teeth were all canines. As I discovered, shortly after he had lit his fire, he was a meat eater and not particularly choosy about where his meat came from. I'd wondered why he had wanted the corpse.

With the fire going the sauraman used a knife to remove one leg from the soldier's corpse. The calf muscle he cut into strips to hang on sticks over the flames. While these were cooking, he separated out the thigh, spitted it, and had it high over the flames to cook through. The strips were done by the time the larger piece of meat began to sizzle and give of the aroma of roasting pork. He ate two or three of the strips before remembering his manners and holding out a stick for me. I demurred, not because of any feeling of disgust, but because my energy source is something that only has to be renewed every five hundred

years. Anyway, he looked hungry. When he insisted I pointed at
myself.

"Collector," I said.

He ate the meat off the end of the stick and then repeated my
name quite precisely. He then pointed to himself.

"Gurt," he said, then he offered me another human satay. He
didn't get it. I'm not so arrogant as to think that everyone on
Earth knows my name and knows what I am. But I've been
around for a long while and it is infrequent that I come across
any who do not. I thought we'd better get things sorted there
and then. I pointed at myself again.

"Cyborg," I said, wondering if he might know the word. He
showed no reaction other than to continue his munching. I
held up my hand, sequenced the release program, then stripped
off the glove of syntheflesh to reveal the skeletal ceramal hand
underneath. Gurt went very still as he looked at my hand. Suddenly he grinned, which was not the reaction I had expected. He
pointed with the stick from my head down to my feet. I did a
partial release at my neck to show ceramal vertebrae and another
to coyly expose the shine at my ankle. He grinned again and
continued with his eating. He didn't offer me any more meat.

The sun flooded the forest with green-filtered light. I listened
to a family of chimpanzees yelling and screaming the order of
the hunt to each other as they tracked and tore apart a spider
monkey. Gurt slept in the shelter of the fallen trees, finally suc-
cumbing after he had chewed the last fragment of flesh from the
thigh bone. The makings of his next meal he had hung in a
nearby tree. I thought him overly optimistic as I listened to hyenas and at least one big cat making their various noises of antici-
pation.

While Gurt slept I watched beetles, their carapaces exactly
matching the fallen elm leaves, bumbling about their business
on the forest floor. I also observed a brown bark mantis watching their activities with a similar if more predatory interest. I do
not need to sleep very much, and when I do it is only for psychological reasons. My brain, flash frozen and bio-gridded, sits inside my ceramal skull unchanging. All those aspects of life that I
have; memory, hate, love, curiosity, are the programs of the syn-
aptic computer linked to that grid. To some it may seem that I
am less than human. I have always felt that I am more.

The synthetic-flesh covering that sheathes my nigh indestructible ceramal skeleton is as sensitive as I wish it to be. I can feel pain, mostly I choose not to. I can feel and sense the world with all the acuity of any man, and more. My vision can range from infrared to ultraviolet and my hearing can extend into ultra and infra-sound. I am as strong a machine as mankind has ever made. I never tire and I never grow thirsty or hungry, yet I can eat and drink and appreciate the experience. My sense of direction sucks though, and I was wondering just then where exactly I was in the forest.

At about midmorning Gurt woke without fuss, drained most of a water bottle, pressed his hand against his stomach, then went off into the forest to attend to a call of nature I had not heard in centuries. The pack of hyenas had drawn closer by then and I heard one of them let off a yelping wail and run yipping into the forest. Gurt, it would seem, was not a man to be overly troubled by the beasts of the wilderness. With his strength, I suspected, he would not be the kind to run for the nearest tree at the sight of a lion. More likely he would eat the lion. Sitting there waiting for him I drained what was left in the water bottle. It looked likely to be a hot day and I might need to sweat for appearance sake.

"Gonna kill 'em," he said, coming back to the fire wiping his hands on a fist full of leaves. This was the first sign from him that he understood my every word.

"Who?" I asked. Perhaps he meant the hyenas.

"God soldiers," he said.

"Ah."

With that he took up two of the opteks and expertly checked their loads. He then strapped one of the pistol belts around himself and filled a bag with spare ammunition for all three weapons.

"Coming?" he asked, when he was ready.

I went and got the APW and a spare power pack, then I followed him into the forest. Now, I thought, it's time I learnt something about him.

"You're a sauraman," I said.

He grunted in the affirmative.

"Are there many more like you?"

"Three," said he.

"Not many."

"Were nine."

"The God soldiers?"

"Killed 'em."

As you may have gathered, extracting facts from Gurt was akin to extracting teeth from a crocodile, yet, despite his monosyllabic replies, I read into him a degree of sophistication. He had accepted me immediately, and he handled weapons with skill and familiarity. I don't mean to say I thought him from some apparently civilised society like that of the families. I think he was that most precious of individuals; an intelligent savage.

We made about half the return distance before Gurt halted and sniffed the air. Wondering precisely what it was he had noticed I upped the sensitivity of my nose. Immediately I picked up the smell of burning wood overlaid with the tang of petroleum. Camp fire, I thought. I couldn't have been more wrong. We moved on more cautiously, Gurt showing more caution than myself. He halted a second then a third time. On the third occasion, he climbed a tree to scout-out our path. He came down the tree very fast.

"Fire," he said.

I was about to offer some sarcastic remark in return when I heard the explosions. As we stood there below the tree he had just quit, two springboks went hurtling past us, closely followed by a lioness. Shortly after them, came a family of chimpanzees, some on the ground and some in the trees. There were no pursuers here; they were all running. Beyond them I saw the wall of fire and concluded that the explosions were exploding trees. Taking a leaf out of Gurt's book of meaningful communication I was reduced to monosyllables.

"Run," I said, about a second after Gurt had already shown me his heels.

Gurt was impressively strong and dangerous in a fight, but one thing he was not was a sprinter. Had this been an ordinary forest fire I think he might have managed to outrun it, but as it was being encouraged along with liberal doses of napalm and oxygen bombs he wasn't fast enough. I accelerated past him and twenty yards ahead I halted, and pushing my APW round to my front on its strap, I pointed a thumb at my back. He didn't hesitate. He discarded the opteks and leapt straight on my back when he reached me. Such was his weight that he even had me staggering for a moment before I corrected. I started off at a steady fifteen kilometres an hour to get used to the load and steadily built it up. Shortly I was up to thirty kilometres an hour, then forty. I passed a couple of chimpanzees, one carrying her baby on her back just as I was carrying Gurt. I clipped another one that chose the wrong moment to leap from tree to tree in front of me and after it had picked itself up it screeched along behind me for a moment before I out-distanced it. Vicious little bastards, but then what can you expect from man's nearest relation?

"Faster," said Gurt, and I imagined that I could feel the heat on the back of my neck.

I accelerated, feeling heat build up in my joints because of the extra loading. I turned on my sweat glands, and they used the water I had drunk earlier. Forty kilometres an hour, forty-five. A bird bounced off my chest and Gurt caught it as it fluttered past. I thought this a rather unreasonable time to be taking a snack.

The fire was soon far behind us and I was able to slow and put Gurt down. From there we continued on at the kilometre-eating trot he seemed able to maintain.

"How wide?" he asked, gesturing at the trees.

"Thirty kilometres," I guessed.

He grunted and we just kept going. An hour later I had to carry him ahead of the flames again. An hour after that I did it again. By midafternoon, just ahead of a pall of smoke and amongst the fleeing animals, we reached the abrupt edge of the forest and the deep hissing stutter I instantly recognised.

I suppose I should have expected something like this. My excuse is that I just got caught up in the excitement of the moment. I had even, momentarily, forgotten all about my precious tree orchids. Why, I should have asked myself, would people who had come to harvest the trees, set fire to the forest? They'd done it to drive someone out of the forest, or at least to remove that someone's cover. It was all about me. I try moderately hard not to be conceited, but this was the only conclusion to which I could come. The weaponry was the decider. You don't position a number of AG gun ships, armed with pulsed-energy cannons, on the edge of a forest to nail an escaped slave or two.

"Shit," I said, monosyllabically.

"Agreed," said Gurt.

The gun ships were square-sectioned stubby crosses, each with a spherical cockpit on the end of one of the arms. On the arms either side of the cockpit were sideways projecting gun turrets adapted to support pulsed-energy cannons. There were no markings on them, but they were standard corporate family manufacture. The question was; which family? It was not a question I felt inclined to consider for overlong when one of those cannons turned on us and opened fire.

The pulsed-energy cannon works on much the same principle as the quantum cascade or QC laser. The laser, developed originally for the solid state electronics' industry a couple of millennia back, was soon taken up by the military when a power pack was invented that could support it as a weapon. These lasers produce coherent light, usually at the red end of the spectrum. The pulsed-energy cannon produces coherent radiations inclusive of X-rays and microwaves. One pulse looks like a tracer bullet. Where it hits it leaves nothing but radioactive ash. It is not a clean weapon, but it is certainly an effective one.

We crawled then ran back into the forest with trees exploding behind us and the whole forest burning ahead of us. Things had taken a decided turn for the worse and it was perhaps this that returned to me, if but for a moment, an at least workable sense of direction. I pointed to our left and held my arms so Gurt could remount. I then ran as fast as I could; forest burning to my right and gun ships blasting away the trees to my left. I could have just buried myself in the earth to wait for it all to be over. There was though the nagging suspicion that whoever was hunting me would be wise to that trick and that there would be Soldiers of God out with metal detectors once the fire had finished. Also, I didn't want to abandon Gurt; he was one genotype I didn't have in my collection, and anyway, I liked him.

The forest floor soon began to slope downhill and I had to slow my headlong rush as the ground got softer. Prairie elms were soon replaced by other deciduous trees like oaks and horse chestnut. You got a curious mix this near to the glacier. The weather is such that old Africa is much encroached on by the temperate climate that had been farther north before the meteor strike and subsequent ice age. Patches of forest like this had sprung up soon after, in the dryer veldt, fed by melt water and cooled by cold air flowing down off the ice. Soon we reached an area of fallen trees where the ground had become too soft to support them and I had to put Gurt down. We made our way through this wreckage to an abrupt stand of bamboo seemingly colonised wholly by giant snails and the adapted land crabs that fed upon them. Beyond the bamboo was swamp that the fire had yet to reach. Gurt looked askance at the water and sphagnum bogs then looked up as one of the gun ships passed overhead scattering fire in every direction. I waded in and he followed.

Night had fallen by the time we reached the river. Using a narrow-beam setting on the APW I cut a tree to raft us downstream. I can't swim, and walking along the bottom gets a bit tedious. I also tend to end up going the wrong direction when I try that. As we floated downstream in darkness I had to discourage one crocodile with a rap on its nose, but otherwise we were okay. A gun ship crossed the river upstream of us with its searchlight probing the water. It had missed us by half an hour or so, for which I was grateful. I had no doubt it was rigged-out with detectors suitable for picking up human-sized lumps of ceramal. Still in darkness we paddled ashore and got out on a muddy bank below the open veldt. I listened to a passing herd of mammoth up there, while Gurt slept curled in the mud, oblivious to the world. I decided then that I needed information and there were those who would be with the mammoth who could provide it. Leaving Gurt to sleep I climbed the bank and set out through the waist-high elephant grass.

A dark shape rested in the stunted branches of a baobab and with glinting eyes watched me approach. He was about to fly until I pulled the glove of syntheflesh off my hand and held up that hand in greeting. The Pykani settled down and waited until I was under the tree.

"I am honoured, Collector," said a lisping voice in the darkness.

"To whom do I speak?" I asked.

"I am Stuka," replied the little vampire in the tree.

Someone, I mention no names, took DNA from the frozen corpse of a mammoth dug from the Russian tundra. From this DNA that someone resurrected the mammoth into a world swiftly being depopulated by water wars, manufactured plagues, and more esoteric killers like the Great African Vampire; creatures bred to feed on people, lots of people. Someone then took DNA from the aforesaid, spliced it with the gene of pygmy humans and produced the Pykani; creatures well adapted to feed upon the blood of the mammoth. Stuka was a perfect little man with a slightly translucent body, bat wings, and fangs.

"An army of God is burning my forest, Stuka," I said.

"We've seen the lights," replied the Pykani.

I looked behind me and I too could see the lights; the long low glow of burning forest and the higher firefly glows of about ten gun ships.

"I think they were after me," I said.

"Their weapons are fearsome."

"Who are they?"

"The Army of God is powerful because it has powerful weapons. They were fanatics without power until someone gave them those weapons. Now their leader styles himself the Lord of Cuberland. You have been named demon and must be destroyed."

"Their weapons?" I asked.

"One of the Families. I do not know which one."

"What about the gun ships?"

"They came only yesterday, Collector."

I thought about that. I thought hard about that. Someone had provided a bunch of fanatics with the weaponry to put them in power. I was now a demon. Sounded like a deal to me: We'll give you these if you off him, we'll also give you back up. A family punch-up with the Army of God as incidental I reckoned. I held sixty percent of the stock in the Jethro Manx Canard Corporation, which made me a viable target either internally or if another family was making a move on Manx Canard. I bet on the latter, as Jethro Susan, my wife of two centuries, had the reins there. I had to get back and find out what was going on. I just wondered what forces would be arrayed to prevent me getting back. I needed more of an edge than was usual for me.

"I require your assistance, Stuka, and that of your tribe," I said.

"You have but to ask, Collector. You are no demon to us," replied the Pykani. I felt a touch of embarrassment at that. In the past I'd let slip that I had been the someone who had resurrected the mammoth and had my status elevated to something angelic as far as the Pykani were concerned. I just hoped they'd never find out who had made them.

A pall of smoke sat in the air above where my forest burned and in that pall flew vultures that had moved in to feast on what charred corpses they could find. The gun ships were absent, which could be a good sign or a bad sign as far as my plans were concerned. When I explained to Gurt he was typically loquacious in giving his opinion.

"We kill them," he said, and grinned.

In the morning we left the river and found a sheltered area underneath a couple of acacias that grew verdant next to a water hole. Gurt lit a fire then went and crouched by the water, still as a heron. I worried about the smoke for a second then dismissed my worries. There was still plenty of smoke in the air. After half an hour Gurt snatched at the water a few times and came back clutching a couple of terrapins. These he opened, beheaded and gutted, then roasted in their shells. The meat had a somewhat adverse effect on him, because thereafter he sat with his stomach grumbling, letting off eructations that were so foul I had to turn off my nose. Perhaps terrapin meat was not the kind he was used to. He had been awfully proficient at cutting up that soldier.

At midday Stuka came gliding in to see me, which surprised me as Pykani are nocturnal. As he landed on the shore of the water hole I saw with even more surprise that he was wearing tight sunglasses. Things move on.

"Little vampire," said Gurt.

"Yes," I said. "Not dinner." Then I went to hear what Stuka had to say.

"It is unusual to see you in the day," I said to Stuka.

"It is unusual to see in the day," replied the vampire. "Jethro Susan has given us much."

"Ah," I nodded my head. My wife, when she had been human, was protected by the vampires and in turn protected the mammoth for them. What developed went by the name of braided debt. I should not have been surprised at the source of these vampire sunglasses. "Good," I stumbled on. "You . . . have news for me?"

"We have located them. They are forty kilometres to the east," said Stuka.

I pointed to where I thought east might be and Stuka corrected me. He then reached into a pouch at his waist and wordlessly handed me the instrument from there. It was a compass. I turned it over and looked at the initials JMCC etched into the back.

"Er, thanks."

When we set out I gave the compass to Gurt to use, and he seemed to manage okay. I found that no matter how I held it it kept pointing at my power supply.

We moved at a steady pace through the elephant grass, or mammoth grass if you like. After half an hour we hit a mam-

moth trail that led in the direction we wanted to go and I naturally speeded up until Gurt began gasping at my side. I slowed to
his pace and kept going. He wasn't built for running distances
at speed. This did not matter too much to me as I soon intended
to find us some transport.

Soon we were heading downhill and the grass was becoming
lusher and interspersed with other vegetation. Large cycads had
been pulled apart by mammoth and an acacia pushed over and
stripped of bark. In the shade of this acacia a lone tigon watched
us pass, but did not pursue. Unlike their close relatives; lions
and tigers, tigons showed enough intelligence to keep well clear
of man. I had found that increased intelligence was often a result of genetic diversification.

We did not catch up with the mammoth, though I guessed we
were close when I saw Pykani roosting on the stubby branches of
a vine-swamped baobab. It was shortly after passing this tree that
we heard the droning of a thruster and watched from cover in
the grass as a gun ship rose into the sky and sped away to the
east. Through the grass we crept towards where the ship had
risen from. Shortly we came upon an area where many trails had
been trodden through the grass and concealment was difficult
to find. From what concealment we could find we observed
three gun ships at rest in a clearing of trampled grass. There was
probably a number of such bases scattered all across the veldt.
Around these ships was an encampment of the Army of God.
There were guards everywhere, and four-man patrols were being
sent out or returning as we watched. I signalled to Gurt and we
moved back into the grass.

"I need a uniform," I said to him once we were out of sight
and hearing of the guards.

"Patrol," said Gurt, with typical brevity.

We moved back to the encampment and watched until one of
those patrols set out. Gurt eagerly moved at a tangent to intercept them and I followed, willing at least in this, to do things his
way. We came upon them fairly quickly and it was only the luck
of the tigon's roar that prevented them seeing us as they all faced
in the direction of that sound. Gurt took position behind a cycad to one side of the narrow trail and I squatted in the grass.
The four men came between us in a neat and disciplined group.
Gurt and I stepped into them simultaneously. I chopped back
into the throat of one man then reached ahead, put one hand
over the front man's forehead, and one hand between his shoul-

der blades, then pushed and pulled simultaneously. I think he was dead before he was even aware of my presence. Gurt felled his two with sharp and very effective blows from the butt of his optek. The two men dropped soundlessly. He stepped past them even as they fell and brought the butt down on the face of the one whose throat I had chopped. It caved his face in and he started to jerk about violently on the ground, bubbling sounds coming from where his face had been. Gurt looked at him with annoyance, then flipped the man over on what was left of his face, laid his optek on the ground, then came down with all his weight on one knee into the man's back. There was a crunch, then more of a crunch when Gurt caught hold of the man's arms and pulled back hard, putting a right angle in the man's back. He lay there quivering, much like his companions, but more messily. I decided not to use his uniform.

After I'd stripped the least soiled uniform from one of the soldiers and placed his mirrored helmet on my head, I helped Gurt conceal the bodies. He wore no uniform as none would fit him. When this was done I took up one of their opteks and passed to Gurt my APW.

"The baobab we passed on the way here," I said and Gurt nodded in recollection. "I'll pick you up there," I said, and headed back to the encampment.

The three Jungers were without family markings or any other identification. For a while I thought that they had been passed on to this Army of God, stripped of any way of retracing. I then saw a young man in light-blue monofilament overalls strolling arrogantly across the encampment, a data console under his arm and a cigarette in his mouth. Whatever corporate family had provided these gun ships had provided pilots as well.

I noted that one of the ships had sections of cowling removed from one arm and two technicians were working away at an AG motor there. I avoided that ship and headed for the one the pilot was strolling towards. As I walked one of the officers noticed me and quickly headed towards me. He was holding out his hand as if he expected me to stop where I was. I ignored him and kept going.

"Soldier, stand!" he shouted.

I stood, not wanting to attract too much attention at that moment. The officer strode up close to me and thrust his face into mine.

"Where the hell do you think you're going?" he hissed at me, a vicious anger in his face. I thought about making some whining excuse, but suddenly that anger was replaced by a momentary confusion, then shock. He did not recognise me. I was not one of his men.

"I'm going to steal one of your gun ships," I said, and drove my fingers full force into his rib cage. The others were too distant to hear the thud as my fingers penetrated between his ribs and into his heart. I closed my hand into a fist around a rib, ripping my fingers through his heart, and held him upright in front of me. Blood gouted from his mouth as he tried to say something more. No one saw. We just looked like officer and soldier facing each other and speaking. Unfortunately the pilot was walking in our direction. I was about to curse Gurt's tardiness when two soldiers on the other side of the clearing turned into screaming pillars of flame and smoke.

Abruptly there was chaos. Soldiers fired at random into the surrounding grasslands, were running to and fro. I saw the technicians hurriedly closing down cowlings on the grounded junger. The pilot broke into a run for the ship to which I was heading. I dropped the officer, and shaking gobbets of heart-flesh from my fingers, I ran for the ship as well. No one noticed. The soldiers were too busy firing at the enemy outside the camp who was intent on frying them all. I reached the door to the craft just behind the pilot. He hit a palm reader to one side of the door then turned towards me as the door slid open.

"What do you think you are doing, soldier?" he asked, every syllable dripping contempt.

I straight armed him through the door and quickly followed him in. The door slid closed behind me and I drove my elbow into the palm lock, effectively sealing the door. He lay gasping on the floor and tried to draw his sidearm. I stamped on his wrist then took his weapon away from him. I didn't want to kill him just yet. While he lay there groaning I reached up, knocked out a ceiling panel and pulled out a ream of optic cable. It was only cable for the computer control systems so there was no problem there. With this I bound his hands behind his back and tied his feet to the bottom of one of the rear compartment seats. Then I stepped into the cockpit.

"What the fuck are you doing!" he shouted. "You can't fly it!"

In the cockpit were three chairs for pilot, navigator, and weapons comp. The latter two could be slaved to the former so the pilot could run all three. In front of the pilot's chair was a touch console with DNA and fingerprint coded pads. All additions and all surplus to requirements. I reached under the console and got hold of another bunch of fibre optics and pulled. The console was mounted on a wide pedestal. I got hold of each side of it, twisted and pulled. Metal ripped and rivets clattered across the decking.

"Jesu!" said the pilot, perhaps realising then who I was.

Exposed in the column was the stub of the original fold-down joystick slaved to servo motors. The joystick was a threedee; in whichever direction you moved it the ship moved, the farther you moved it in any direction the more acceleration you got. It also had a button that put the stick into 'tilt and turn mode'. This was usually used when holding position and straf-ing an area. I pulled it free of the servos to expose the manual fir-ing button. I had no targeting, but wouldn't need it at this range. I sat in the chair, pulled up the joystick, reached down past it, snapped off two servos and pushed across two levers. The AG started with a drone and the thrusters rumbled. I looked out through the screen at the running soldiers and the two other craft. A twitch of the joystick had the gun ship turning towards the ship nearest. I pressed the firing button.

The only things that will stop the blast from a pulsed-energy cannon are powerful ionic fields, and thick ceramal battle ar-mour (the stuff I'm made of, mostly). Ionic fields are normally only installed on large stations. Ceramal battle armour is too heavy for anything that flies. White fire hammered across the clearing and the men in its path were instantly vaporised. That fire traversed one limb of the nearest gun ship, slagging one tur-ret and the motors in that limb, before it hit the cockpit. The cockpit blackened and deformed like a plastic bottle cast into a furnace, then it exploded. The gun ship tilted and slid sideways trailing fire into the grassland. Behind it the other ship was four metres off the ground with its back to me. Still keeping pressure on the fire button I brought my ship higher. The second ship tried to pull away on its thrusters. I hit one of them and the ex-plosion tilted it while the second thruster drove it round in a cir-cle. Continued fire had it raining molten metal all about. Then it dropped like a brick as its AG went offline. I slagged both its turrets then lifted my ship higher. Bullets were pinging off the skin of my ship by then but I had no fear of them. My worry was of one of those soldiers using an APW. I tilted my ship and continued firing. Men were blown to ash and dirty black smoke rose all around. There was no APW fire but that from Gurt. As instructed he had taken out any soldiers armed with an APW. When I finally took my finger off the firing button there was little but smoke and glowing ground below me. Perhaps some of the soldiers had escaped. I could care less.

Gurt waited calmly under the branches of the vine-swamped baobab as I brought the gun ship down on the elephant grass. I walked into the rear section and stepped over the pilot, who looked at me white-faced and silent. The palm-lock for the door I had to rip away so as to get at the lever underneath. Gurt quickly climbed inside after I had opened the door. He looked speculatively at the bound pilot.

"No, not dinner. I've got to ask him a few questions," I said.

Gurt grunted and followed me to the cockpit. The pilot looked at us with stark terror. I hadn't needed to say that, but it would help with the questioning later. I gestured Gurt to the seat for weapons comp and took the pilot's chair again.

"Best we find somewhere secure before some bright spark sends a smart missile or we get a visit from some more gun ships," I said. "You ever been in one of these before?"

"Been in machines," said Gurt, eyeing the screen and controls before him.

"None of that works at the moment. Let's hope we don't need it."

I lifted the junger off the ground then and Gurt gripped his arm rests. At an attitude of a hundred metres I pushed the joystick all the way forwards for maximum thrust. That thrust had us pressed into our seats for a couple of minutes until I eased off. It also had the pilot groaning and swearing from the back. As I slowed the junger and let it cruise on at a steady two hundred kph, Gurt chuckled. I looked at him and saw that he was now completely relaxed in his seat and was looking at the scenery with interest and pleasure.

"It's good up here," he said.

I had to agree, but it wasn't safe. Shortly after he said this the radio crackled to life.

"Seeker ten, this is Homeboy, respond," said a suspicious-sounding individual. I ignored the voice until it went away, which it did, only to return every ten minutes thereafter.

It took one hour to reach my destination. I'd chosen one of my hideaways that was on route to the JMCC complex. I had considered not stopping at all, but felt I was pushing things as it was. To get to the complex in this ship would take me five hours and in that time I felt there was certain to be a reaction from whoever my enemies were. I needed a little unsubtle up-cannoning to get me through, and the thing about being as old as I am, is that you've had time to prepare, for just about anything.

I brought the ship to the base of a cliff that had been shoved up by the Great Convulsion, and traversed along it. It took another quarter of an hour to find the section of cliff I was looking for. I'd burnt meaningless but distinctive marking in the rock. I'd poured dyes in the soil all around and planted the area with dwarf water oaks. My sense of direction and of place had been as bad then as it was now, hence these preparations.

With a thought, I activated a signal device inside my chest as soon as we were in the area. A round buttress of cliff revolved, shedding trees a couple of centuries old as it did so. The entrance exposed was sufficiently large to accommodate the gun ship. I flew it in to the darkness and brought it down. As I did this the revolving buttress closed behind me and lights came on all around. I pointed out of the cockpit screen at the object resting only a few hundred metres away on the stone floor.

"No more flying?" Gurt asked.

"Too dangerous," I said. "It's a family I'm up against and they'll have gun ships with pulsed energy cannons, and smart missiles. This old girl —" I slapped the steering column. "—would end up in very small pieces if I was to take it out."

Gurt grunted and looked out at the tank. It was an ugly indelicate machine. Everything about it was heavy and solid. The tracks were three metres wide and half a metre thick. The tank itself was a boxlike slab twenty metres long by ten wide and five thick. Its main guns were pulsed-energy, like the junger, but it also had a missile launcher, small automatic antipersonnel machine guns, a nice napalm slinger, and a rear turret that operated on a carousel system so I could call up any of a selection of eighteen other weapons. All a bit OTT, but I'd been updating the thing (and its various cousins) for seven hundred years, and there was little I had not thought of. It also had limited AG and a couple of thrusters at the back. It could hop. The best thing

about it was that it was made of ceramal battle armour and had
an ionic field projector.

"We are going to have fun," I said, and stood up.

As we went into the back of the gun ship I squatted by the
bound pilot.

"Now, which Family are you a member of?" I asked him.

He just stared back at me, white-faced and defiant. I reached
down, got hold of his shattered wrist, and gave it a squeeze. He
yelled, but refused to answer my question. Gurt moved up behind me.

"If you hang them by their feet they don't faint when you
skin them," said the sauraman. It was the longest speech I had
heard from him.

"I know," I said, "but sometimes they die before you can get
answers."

"Was never after answers," said Gurt.

The pilot looked wide-eyed at Gurt. I squeezed his wrist again
to get his attention.

"Which family?"

"Fuck you!"

I squeezed again and asked again. It was on about the fourth
occasion that he fainted. I stood up and looked down at him.

"By his ankles," said Gurt.

I nodded then said, "Bring him along. Try not to damage him
too much."

"Skin him now?" Gurt asked.

"No, there's easier and less messy ways. We'll take him to the
complex," I said.

The tank started first with the droning of the hydrogen tur-
bine that got the allotropic uranium up to speed. The batteries
were at full charge as I always kept them and had more than
enough power to get us to the complex, but they'd not last long
if, as seemed highly likely, I started using the energy cannons or
any of the esoteric carousel weapons. Gurt ungently taped the
pilot in the chair for the satcom and wrapped extra tape round
his mouth. I had the sauraman sit in the driver's chair. I sat at
the weapon's console. As in the gun ship, the weapons console
could be slaved to the driver, but I thought Gurt would enjoy
the experience of driving a ceramal battle tank. It seemed just his
sort of thing and it was unlikely he could damage it. I pointed at
the two joysticks.

"One for each tread," I said. "Push them forwards and we go forwards. Pull them back and we go back. One forward and one back and we go in a circle—"

"I understand," Gurt interrupted. He squinted at the grey bulkhead before him.

"That pad there," I said and pointed at the touch pad clearly labelled 'front screen'. He hit the pad harder than necessary and the bulkhead effectively disappeared as the front screen came on. He grinned out at the interior of the cave and tightly gripped the sticks.

"When we get out of the cave head south south-east," I said, pointing at the face of the gyrocompass. "Try not to knock over too many trees and avoid large boulders." I sent the signal to the door in the cliff and it revolved open. Gurt thrust forward with the controls and with a rumbling drone the tank surged forwards. As we came out into the sunlight I hit another screen button and the ceiling, side walls, and rear bulkhead disappeared. It was almost as if we were riding on an open platform. Gurt grunted and looked about in surprise, then he grinned at me with delight. He seemed to be adapting to the technology very quickly. I grinned back at him then put radar, laser bounce, and air perturbation detectors online. Gurt immediately drew back on the joysticks and brought the tank down to a crawl when faced with the forest of dwarf water oaks. He looked an enquiry at me.

"Take us through," I said. He looked for some sort of track, saw none, shrugged and pushed the sticks forward. The tank hit the trees at about twenty kph and did not slow. Trees shattered before it and rode up over the roof. The tank lifted a little over some of the bigger stumps where trees broke off, but mostly the trees were torn right out of the ground and shoved aside. The noise was hideous until I muted it. We were in a chaos of shattered wood and branches for about five minutes before we broke out onto an upslope. Small boulders on the slope broke with dull explosions under the treads. At the head of the slope we rode up then came down with a crash on level veldt thick with elephant grass.

"Open her up," I instructed, most of my attention on the detectors. Gurt pushed the sticks all the way forwards and the tank accelerated to its full speed of eighty kilometres per hour. From the grass came a constant hiss as of fire and it built up in clumps on the front of the tank before riding up over the roof. I kept watching the detectors.

At fifty kilometres and about one kilometre up I had four signatures. The computer decoded them and flung up a schematic of a junger gun ship in the corner of the screen. There was no concerted movement from them for ten minutes. They seemed to be following a search pattern. Then as one they started to come in our direction. A quarter of an hour and they would be on us. I guessed they wouldn't attack right away as they had no idea who was in this tank. I also guessed that someone higher up the chain of command would have an idea and eventually order an attack. I had the computer target the ships at that extreme range and selected the missile launcher. I put the shield on auto and diverted half of the power from the U-charger to its laminar storage capacitor. As they only carried energy cannons they would not be able to attack until close in. The tank slowed as soon as I did this and Gurt looked at me.

"Nothing to worry about," I told him, watching the detectors for a moment longer before selecting the scope. It had just occurred to me that there was an outside chance that these were friends and it just wouldn't do to go shooting them out of the sky. I used the laser bounce to sight and focus, as the gun ships had a coating that made them invisible to radar. Shortly I had a picture on my screen of the four ships. Like the one back in the cave and the ones I had destroyed, these were without markings. My hand paused over the launch control and I felt a twinge of guilt. Damned if I know why. I yielded to this and selected only one missile. Then I tapped the launch control.

As if by magic the missile launcher appeared suspended over our heads. It turned and spat a single missile from the side of its post-box launching mouth. That missile shot away without pause for acceleration. Its engine ignited when it was some distance towards the horizon. The launcher operated as a mini rail gun to sling the missiles out. It had been discovered in a war some centuries back that the pause for acceleration in the old style missiles had allowed enough time for a laser to target, and missiles had often been detonated only a few metres from their launcher. The launcher disappeared from the overhead screen and I called up the scope picture again to watch the show. Gurt slowed the tank so he could watch as well.

The four gun ships were cruising at full speed about fifty metres above the ground. Abruptly one of them tilted and turned violently. The pilot must have picked up on the incoming at the last moment. He did not move his ship quickly enough. The missile went in so fast it showed only as a flicker of a line on the screen. The explosion gutted the ship with fire, blasting out through its four limbs before disintegrating it completely. Red-hot hull plates and distorted structural members rained out of the sky. To one side I observed a thruster motor, still firing intermittently, hit the ground and disappear in a hot blue explosion. The other gun ships had gone into avoidance manoeuvres and the screen tracked on only one of them. I clicked on the radio.

"Consider that warning enough. Come no closer," I said.

On the laser bounce detector I observed the three remaining ships pull away and hold at a distance ten kilometres out from where I had destroyed that one. No doubt they were asking for instructions and hoping the instructions they received were not; "Go in."

"They're going to need a sieve to find what's left of you Mr Collector," someone hissed at me over the radio. Checking a couple of readings I could see that I had screen or holovisual if I wanted them. I selected screen and looked into the angry face of one of the gun ship pilots. He was angry at me. The cheek.

"Ah, a talkative one," I said. "Your friend doesn't say much." The pilot looked confused so I turned the screen so he could see my prisoner over my shoulder. His confusion went away.

"You bastard," he said.

"That's hardly fair," said I. "I didn't start this. Perhaps if you tell me what this is all about we can sort things out amicably."

The pilot shut off communication and I turned to Gurt.

"Keep us moving. I think the shit's about to hit."

Gurt immediately understood the ancient euphemism and had us pelting across the veldt as fast as the tank could manage. I got all my detectors online and watched for movement. I was tempted to take out the three remaining gun ships but thought that might be a waste of missiles of which I might have sore need. The tank only carried fifty after all. As we hurtled along I observed more blips on the screen, which the computer identified as more gun ships. It also informed me that some of these gun ships were carrying missiles.

"Why you waiting?" Gurt asked, and for the life of me I had no answer for him. Perhaps I was getting soft in my old age. I quickly targeted the ships with missiles and launched. I think fingers must have hit firing buttons simultaneously because as my missiles sped away the computer picked up on incoming.

"Ah," I said, and made a selection on the carousel. It was something I'd always wanted to try. At the back of the tank the carousel whirred and clicked and an object like an iron camera thunked up into position, tracked, and fired. The muted sound that came from it was as of escaping compressed air. It tracked again, fired again and again. The object's title was MMG, which stood for mega-multigun. It fired ceramic bullets five millimetres across at a rate of one million per minute. There was not much else as effective at stopping missiles. I watched my screen and saw approaching missiles disappearing. I also noted that the same was happening at the other end but not as effectively. My missiles were being brought down by lasers. Three got through and three gun ships disappeared from the screen. One of their missiles, obviously with its targeting out, hit about ten metres from the tank. The blast slewed us sideways and a sheet of fire and debris momentarily covered us. Gurt got the tank back in line and kept us moving forwards. On my screen I got an error message and looked up at the multigun. It was gone.

"Fuck," I said, called up the laser from the carousel, and activated the ionic screen. I launched two more batches of missiles as the remaining gun ships with missiles launched theirs. Suffice to say that after that exchange they no longer had the capability of firing missiles at me. The tank, unfortunately dropped to a power level that shut off the engine, and we sat there in the burning elephant grass with the U-charger whining at full load as it struggled to restore power. I should have expected what happened next.

"Collector, you are an anachronism and a pain," said someone, and I noted that there was no visual transmission. I waited and the voice continued. "Admittedly you're resourceful, but in the end your resources are limited. I would guess that right now you're running out of energy."

I looked at the screen and noted that the gun ships were pulling away. I'd expected tactical nukes next and reckoned I had enough armament to field them. It didn't look like that was going to be the next. I thought fast and came up with only one conclusion. I pulled up the microphone and held it in the palm of my hand, then I leant across and set Gurt's joysticks to drive. As soon as the U-charger had stacked up enough power in the batteries the tank would take off. I looked Gurt in the eye and nodded towards the door. When he sat there looking puzzled I turned the microphone off.

"Get out and run. I'll be with you in a moment. No questions," I said, and turned the microphone back on. Gurt got out of his seat and picked up the APW and a hand gun. He opened the door, leapt out, and set out into the burning grass land at his steady loping pace.

"Who am I speaking to?" I asked as I quickly set the defence and weapons systems on automatic.

"What does that matter to you now?" the voice asked, relishing his victory.

I was out of my seat and through the door in a moment, the microphone still in my hand. My captive watched me go with stark terror in his features. I guessed he knew what was coming.

"Look, I'm carrying enough armament to take out anything you've got. Perhaps we should discuss this. What do you want of me?"

By this time I was running into the grassland after Gurt. One of the advantages of not having to breath is that you can talk quite calmly while making like an Olympic sprinter.

"What I want of you, Collector, is your absence. Goodbye."

I was about a hundred metres from the tank and fast catching up with Gurt when I heard the tank start moving. It's all very well rolling across the veldt in a high tech battle tank, but there comes a point when you begin to think you're invulnerable. That is something you should never think and was the kind of attitude that had got a lot of my kind dead. Behind me the tank started discharging its load of missiles. The carousel was operating as well, shooting out the black erratically flying spheres of smart bombs. I reckoned a few more gun ships would bite the dust before it was all over.

The sound was like the sea and the entire area was bathed in crimson light. I came up behind Gurt and brought him down to protect his body with mine. There was a brief roaring as the ionic shield came full on for a moment then collapsed. At that moment I crushed the microphone I held, then, with my eye shutters up to filter radiations that might damage my more delicate optics, I turned my head and looked back. The armour went from red to white in an instant then the tank exploded flinging chunks of ceramal in every direction. The smoke and fire picked out the shape of the laser beam like a nacreous column rising into the sky. It bored into the ground for a moment then shut off. Where my tank had been was now a crater lined with cooling glass. I rolled off Gurt and allowed him to sit upright.

"You won't question him now," he said.

For a moment I didn't know what he was talking about, then I remembered the pilot I had left in the tank. I tried to feel some sympathy for the man, but all that came out was a snort as I tried to suppress a laugh.

"He not there anymore," said Gurt.

That did it. I cracked and sat laughing with ash and smoke swirling about me. Gurt looked at me in his puzzled way for a moment then he too started to laugh. Eventually we staggered to our feet and headed away from the burning area. It was only at nightfall when we sat at a fire, over which Gurt roasted half a springbok downed by shrapnel, that he asked me what had happened.

"Some of the families have weapons in orbit. That was the blast from a satellite sun laser," I explained.

"Sun laser?" he asked.

I wondered if he would understand. I did my best to explain.

"A laser beam is coherent light . . . light that has all its photons travelling in parallel. It's usually generated by crystals that lase, like rubies . . ."

"Ruby laser," Gurt said.

"Yes . . . A sun laser is a huge solar collector that focuses sunlight into one point. At that point is something called a cohering field which does the same job as a ruby, but in one hit. No material object would stand the temperatures involved. Sun lasers were used in some of the big engineering projects." I pointed at the half moon that showed part of the labyrinthine bases on its face. "They used them to bore the lunar caverns and to smelt the asteroids for the materials to build bases."

Gurt stared at the moon as if seeing it for the first time. I realised then that I had been right about him: He was an intelligent primitive. He had a huge ability to learn, and to absorb information. Obviously until now he'd had few sources of information and no teachers. I decided I should take on those roles.

"Where do you come from, Gurt?" I asked.

"Ankatra," he enlightened me.

"Where is that from here?"

He pointed vaguely southeast.

"How far?" I asked with infinite patience.

"Don't know. We in machines and rooms and I falling," he said.

I took that in and chewed it over. 'Falling' inclined me to think Gurt had at some point been in a space craft or on a station.

"What happened in the rooms?"

"They studied us. They took bits of us away. They wanted to see how strong and how fast we were. Horl showed then. He killed one of them. They burned him."

"What then?"

"We went to sleep and woke up in a pen. We escape in the night then God soldiers find us and shoot at us. I escape then caught and God soldiers keep me. I escape again."

I had a sudden intimation of what might be going on.

"How many of you at the colony?" I asked.

"Many thousand," Gurt answered proudly. It was obviously a number he had only recently mastered.

"What was it like there?"

"We fighting all the time about lemu rights."

"Lemu rights?"

"Meat."

Oh hell.

"Do you have another name for this colony?" I asked.

"Gascar," he replied.

I sat back and thought about that one. The last time I had been to Madagascar there had only been a few widely-spaced human settlements. That had been four centuries ago. Someone had obviously made a few changes there since. I considered all that had happened in the light of his story. Perhaps I had been arrogant to assume that the family gun ships had been sent to dispose of me. It sounded to me like someone had been running a secret project, had loused, then sent the ships in to clean up. My meeting Gurt had obviously been a large spanner in the works. Now, whoever had been running that project, thought myself and the sauraman dead. We had to get to JMCC. I had to find out what the hell was going on.

Gurt learned fast. Over the next few days I spoke non-stop on any subject that took my interest, and anything I thought might be of interest to him. As we walked I would point out a ruin and give him a potted history, or I would point out a genetically adapted plant and do the same. I told him about the Pykani and the mammoth and one night when a devil shriek echoed down from the sky I told him about the Great African vampires. More and more often he asked questions, and his questions rapidly gained coherence.

"Why did the ice come?" he asked me one evening.

"That was a big surprise for everyone. I told you about the resource wars and how the Corporations took power from the Governments?"

"You did."

"Well, it was the Corporations that got us into space. They knew that Earth was getting used up. With the fossil fuels down to their last dregs they knew we'd soon not have the resources for a concerted space-effort, and that we'd end up trapped on Earth and knocked back into the Stone Age by repeated environmental disasters. They made the effort and got us into space, leaving Earth to its steady global warming. That global warming was well underway when a comet completed its twenty-thousand year orbit and struck, right in the middle of what was then called America—there's nothing but volcanic islands there now. The debris flung up brought about a darkness that lasted long enough to kill two thirds of life on Earth. The humans and animals that survived, walked out into the beginning of an ice age. Earth's orbit had been perturbed enough to bring that about."

Gurt quietly digested this then the questions started. I had to tell him about the Stone Age, America, what Earth's orbit was, and what fossil fuels were. When the conversation got onto fossils I made the mistake of mentioning dinosaurs and his relation to them. That conversation led on to basic genetics. He wanted to know so much and I was forced to ask him just how much of this he was remembering. This question puzzled him. I quizzed him about some things I had told him the day before and he recited them back at me verbatim. I realised then that he, like myself, did not have the capacity to forget. He took in knowledge sponge-like. Some of the words he might not understand, but he would not forget them and eventually he would find something to which he could apply them.

On our fourth day of travel we reached JMCC. The ground complex squatted on the plain like a huge metallic crab. It was five kilometres in diameter, but less than half a kilometre in height. Windows below the smooth dome of the roof glinted like beady eyes. Off to one side, partially hidden by the complex, was the fenced-off landing field, a scattering of control towers, and two behemoths of flying-wing shuttles. To the people of Earth the corporate families are notoriously reclusive. This is only because they had no great interest in Earth. Their interests are in the space above it. As we walked towards the complex I explained this to Gurt and he asked me what precisely were their interests. I told him wealth, power, pleasure; no different to the interests of Earth people. When we were about a kilometre out, an AG ground car shot out towards us. Things had changed somewhat since that time I came here carrying Jethro Susan's dying human body, before going off to hunt down a body for her much like my own. Then, JMCC were using wheeled ground cars driven by diesel engines. This had been the result of a slow decline in their fortunes and the loss of certain technologies. Because of me they had those technologies back now.

The car drew to a halt before us, its doors hissed open, and a man and a woman in monofilament coveralls stepped out. Both of them were helmeted and carried QC laser carbines. The woman spoke first.

"Who are you and what do you want?" she asked, eyeing Gurt. I, of course, looked completely human and did not have an APW strapped across my back.

"I'm the Collector," I said.

She looked at me without disbelief and centred the snout of her laser on my chest.

"I'll be needing proof of that of course," she said.

Internally I sent a signal to a superconductor nerve nexus. The nerve interlinks to my left hand autodetached. It went numb. I reached across and pressed the two pressure points to break the seal then I stripped off my hand covering. I held up the skeletal hand of ceramal, which is mostly what I'm made of.

"You have to understand, if you are who you say you are, that I'll need more proof than that. Twenty years ago then Enmarks sent an agent here with a ceramal arm. He passed himself off as the Collector for three days and did a lot of damage before Jethro Susan came back from her tour of the orbital stations and he was found out...'" She pointed to a distant acacia. "We nailed him there."

"Oh well," I said, reaching up to my neck and pressing a sequence of soft spots. Another internal signal caused interlinks to detach. The synthetic muscle that gave my face expression detached as well. My face went dead and still. I pulled it off.

It was a good trick that I'd done many times. The expressions of the two went from calm competence to a species of sick fear. I turned and grinned at Gurt—I wasn't capable of any other expression at that moment—and he grinned back. I think he was faking it a bit.

"That's . . . fairly conclusive," said the man.

The woman said nothing for a moment, then, "We'll bring you to Jethro Susan. She will know for sure. First I'll have that APW please . . . Collector."

I nodded to Gurt and he handed the weapon over. We got into the ground car and they took us into the complex. Sometimes it bugs me what I have to go through just to prove who I am, but I guess passport photos and fingerprints are out of the question.

It was eighty years since I had last spoken to Jethro Susan. We'd got along fine for about forty years then we'd just drifted apart as she developed interests in JMCC, of which she had been a part from the beginning, and I went back to my collecting and, as she put it, "Playing your lethal little games." There was no particular acrimony between us, nor did we have any great interest in each other. I had no wish to lord it in JMCC and live mostly enclosed in metal. I like the wildernesses of Earth. I had always liked them. Earth was mine. Since we had gone a separate ways some hundred and sixty years ago we had met on and off about once every twenty years. Either she came to find me to get my deciding vote on some JMCC policy decision, or I returned to the complex for equipment, and on an occasion when a bounty hunter came after me with an atomic shear, for repairs. The last time I came in had been to use the laboratories to grow orchids from a speck of DNA I had extracted from an ancient bottle of perfume, and thence from them to obtain seeds. It was those orchids that I established in my forest.

Susan was home this time. On the last occasion she come down in a shuttle to confirm my identity. As the lift took us up to the Corporate boss' apartments I felt slightly anxious about meeting her. Gurt was back to his usual apparent reserve, but I could see his eyes darting about as he took everything into that wonderfully absorbent brain of his. The doors opened and we walked in with the guards either side of us. Susan stood up from behind a desk that was a slab of petrified wood polished to a sheen and supported in a thick water-oak frame. She gestured at the guards.

"You may leave us," she said.

"Are you sure . . .? " asked the woman.

"I'm sure. If anyone was to turn up now, with a sauraman, I'd have expected it to be him," she said wearily.

I looked around at the room.

"You've redecorated," I said inanely.

The circular chamber had been floored with soft-screen tiles set to react to pressure. From each step I took ripples of coloured light spread out across the floor. From me there were more ripples than from Gurt or the guards, but then I weighed as much as them all together. Behind one glassed wall had been mounted the preserved body of a female GAV with her wings spread in flight and her fangs exposed in a snarl, at least I assume she was the real thing and not merely a projected image. Behind the desk was a panoramic window with a view over the curve of the dome and out over the landing field. As we walked in I observed a heavy lifter rising under the impetus of AG, then tilting when it was high up and accelerating away with a blast of thrusters that put a blue flame halfway across the sky.

The guards backed into the lift and the doors slid closed on them. I advanced to one of the tubular glass chairs before the desk and sat down. The chair creaked alarmingly, but managed to take my weight. Gurt looked slightly unsure of himself for a moment, then he quickly walked forward and sat in another of the chairs. Susan sat back down in her chair and put her feet on her desk. She looked good; long black hair hanging loose, elfin face with azure eyes, and a lean and boyish figure. But then, she could look just how she liked. She could build up an image of the body and face she wanted in her computer, sent it down to the synthetics department, and have a new body covering ready for her in a couple of days. Underneath she was like me; a skeleton of ceramal filled with hardware that was ancient, yet state-of-the-art, as the art had yet to be improved on.

"Well?" she asked me.

"There's an Army of God out there that considers me a demon. There's thousands of sauramen living on Madagascar. Gurt here is an escapee from some sort of family study or assessmentof his kind. Me and him have been ducking APWs, gun ships, and one satellite strike over the last week or so. How are things with you?" I said.

She looked very carefully at Gurt and ignoring my sarcasm said, "Family project?"

"I'd have thought so, and the quantity of them tells us something as well," I said.

"A private army," said Susan, noncommittal.

Gurt was looking from one to the other of us. I expected him to say something, but he just watched and listened.

"The question is; which family?" I said.

Just then the lift door opened and in walked a short ugly man carrying a large tray. He stopped in the middle of the floor, the ripples now spreading out from his feet looking exactly like ripples on water. Susan nodded to the end of her desk nearest to Gurt. The man walked there and placed the tray on the desk. It was loaded with fancy foods. Gurt looked at the tray and his stomach rumbled loudly. The man stood by the desk waiting.

"Drinks, anyone?" Susan asked.

"Beer. Same for Gurt," I said.

Susan nodded at the man and he went on his way. She gestured at the food.

"Please, help yourselves."

Gurt pulled his chair forwards, picked up a chicken leg, sniffed it then shoved it in his mouth. He ate it all, crunching up the bone as well, then he steadily began working his way across the tray. I didn't bother with anything. I do have a sense of taste and can be hungry if I so wish. The pleasure of eating is there for me if I want it, but when that pleasure is infrequently reinforced it ceases to be of interest. Susan had yet to get out of the habit. She nibbled at a vol-au-vent and watched Gurt with amusement.

"Do you have any idea which family it might be, then?" I asked again.

Still watching Gurt eat, Susan said, "Over the last month we've lost to sabotage a factory and two comsats. This sort of thing hasn't happened in three centuries. I would say our problems are related."

I leant back and looked at the ceiling, aware she hadn't really answered my question. I wondered what she might be concealing from me: She'd had a more-or-less free hand at JMCC for the last century and a half.

"Molly, which family's sun laser was used four days ago against the surface of Earth?"

The smooth sexy voice of a woman I had known more than a thousand years ago, replied, "The sun laser used has long been listed as an historical monument under joint family ownership."

Gurt looked up at the ceiling, looked around the room, grunted and shoved another chicken leg in his mouth.

"Is there any way of finding out who used it?" I asked.

Susan replied, "There isn't. It's already been looked into. Someone had obviously kept the laser secretly online for a long time for . . . eventualities. There's no trail to follow."

"That eventuality was one of my battle tanks," I said.

"Poor boy," said Susan.

"Ask the God Soldiers," said Gurt.

We both looked at him, but he thereafter ignored us and continued with his munching.

"Well, someone provided them with weapons and piloted gun ships," I said.

"You should have snatched one of the pilots," said Susan.

"I did, but I left him in the tank."

"Remiss of you. We'll send people in, get another one then, or a military adviser, something."

"No, I'll go in," I said.

Susan shook her head.

"Killing you is just a way of destabilising JMCC; just a preparatory move before a strike. Why put yourself in that kind of danger? I've got professional people here who can do this."

"If you give me cover I won't be in much danger. I know another satellite strike is unlikely now, but I want that small likelihood covered."

"You'll be taking out another of those blasted tanks?"

"Oh yes."

Our conversation was interrupted by Susan's servant bringing in another tray. On this were bottles of beer and thin beakers made of artificial pearl. He poured us each a drink from one of the large bottles then quickly retreated. I had to ask.

"Servants, Susan? Are you over-budgeted on manpower?"

"Jank is not a man. He's my protection."

"Android?"

Susan shrugged. She wasn't telling. I let it drop.

"I've got another store over near the border of Cuberland. I'll run out there in a wing and take it from there. I suggest you prepare for attack," I said.

"Already underway. Since the sabotage we've been expecting something," she replied.

"Satellite strike?"

"Even now I have platforms moving into the ionosphere. You'll be covered."

I sipped at my beer. I needed liquids as coolants and beer was as good a liquid as any other. On my second sip I remembered to turn on my taste buds and as always, was pleasantly surprised at the unaccustomed input. Gurt watched me for a moment then picked up a beaker. After his first taste he looked with suspicion into the beaker before taking another sip.

"I'd also suggest you let it be generally known about Gurt's people on Madagascar. Once that's done everyone will be watching," I said, and turned to Gurt. "What do you want, Gurt?"

"I want to kill God soldiers," he enunciated perfectly.

I hadn't expected any different.

The wing was just a two-man transport, with AG, an array of thrusters, and a single steering wing mounted underneath. It was the fastest way of getting from point A to B in atmosphere. By the time Gurt and I reached the landing field it was fuelled and ready for me on the glassite surface. Gurt was walking a little unsteadily. He'd told me he had not liked the beer to begin with. It seemed to me that he soon acquired the taste. He'd emptied two of the two-litre bottles while Susan and I made our plans.

I lifted the wind on AG, hit the thrusters, and in seconds we were out over the veldt. It took less than an hour to cover the distance it had taken us four days to cover on foot. At extreme detector range I picked up on four gun ships heading for the Atlas mountains. I ignored them and turned east towards Cuberland. Below us the veldt was swiftly encroached on by ambatch trees, acacia scrub, and scattered groundsels. There were river valleys down there where bamboo and cycad forests fought their slow war. Into some of these valleys were the crushed-plant highways of mammoth trails, and on one occasion we passed over a herd of some three hundred mammoth. I turned to Gurt to point this out, but he was fast asleep. It seemed he did not remain long impressed by anything.

Another hour brought me over a river valley, in which the red-stained ground had been planted with dwarf water-oaks. Sometime someone was going to make the connection. I reversed thrusters and decelerated into the valley. Gurt snorted and looked round blearily. He sat up and looked down at the wide, slow-flowing river below us. I brought the wing down until it was ten metres above the surface and we could clearly see the crocodiles lying like logs washed up on the banks, and a single completely pink hippo charging into a bamboo thicket. With a couple of bursts from the thrusters I had us travelling upstream to the inevitable cave from which the river issued. As we slid into the shadows, swarms of bats thumped against the screens. So thick a swarm was it that the wing slowed. I hit the lights and waited for it to clear. When it finally did I gave us another little boost from the thrusters.

The cave went deep under the land. After about two hundred metres the river dropped away below and I brought the wing down on a stone floor mounded with bat droppings and crawling with cockroaches.

"This is it," I said to Gurt.

He looked askance at me as I got out, but he followed.

In the dark I used infrared and Gurt his saurian vision. Carrying weapons we'd brought from JMCC we walked between the swarming mounds to a wall of the cave. I didn't know precisely where the door was so I sent the signal from there. The stone-effect door ground open about ten metres to my right. Bat droppings, cockroaches, and a couple of foot-long centipedes dropped into the lighted lift. Great. We'd brought along a couple of APW carbines, QC handguns, some explosives and a pack of supplies for Gurt. What we hadn't brought was a shovel. I walked up to the lift drawing my QC gun. On wide beam I fried everything living in the lift. I didn't want my hideaway crawling with cockroaches. I do have some standards. Using our feet Gurt and I kicked most of the bat droppings out of the lift. Once we were inside, the door grated shut and the lift immediately took us up. Let it suffice for me to say that a few hours later Gurt was at the controls of another of my tanks and we were crossing into Cuberland.

It soon became evident that we were entering the territory of the Army of God when Gurt brought the tank onto a dirt track through the acacia shrub. At regular intervals along the edge of the road were stakes on which had been impaled those guilty of infractions of the severe religious laws here. Soon we came to a wooden gate across this road and a small guard outpost. I decided it was time to ask directions.

"You stay in here," I instructed Gurt.

"I don't want to," he said.

Four guards had come out of the outpost and were standing looking at the tank, unsure about what to do next. I decided I would use a more indirect approach than was usual for me.

"Okay," I said to Gurt. "Stand back from me and don't kill anyone unless it becomes necessary. We're after information here."

We climbed out of the tank and walked over to the guards. Gurt carried his APW and his laser. I only carried a laser.

"Good evening," I said to the one I ascertained to be the leader here. He was a tall fair-skinned man with long blond hair under his mirrored helm. His three companions were bushmen. One of them, by the marking on his face, looked to be a Yoruba tribesman. The soldier looked at me impassively.

"I was wondering if you could help me." I gestured back to the tank. "I have here a gift for the Bishop, but I seem to have become lost." Really lame.

"Papers," said the soldier, holding out his hand. His three companions had their opteks pointed at us. I continued walking until I was up against the gate. They stood a couple of metres away on the other side of it.

"Paper? No one said anything about papers," said I.

"Remove your weapons and drop them on the ground, now," said the soldier. So much for all my good intentions. I reached down, heaved the gate up, and threw it at them, then I drew my laser. They all went down in an ungainly heap under the heavy gate. One optek discharged its box into the sky. Gurt stepped past me and burnt a hole through the Yoruba's face.

"Leave one alive," I said, holstering my weapon again. Gurt stamped hard on the chest of one of the remaining bushmen then burnt a hole through the throat of the other. The fair-skinned one had by then scrabbled out from under the gate and was reaching for the pistol in his belt. Gurt kicked his legs out from under him, swatted him on the side of his head with the flat of his hand, then removed the pistol from his slack grip. I'd been worried about Gurt getting hurt. I'd forgotten how he had performed in the forest.

"Check that," I said to him, gesturing to the outpost. He nodded and trotted towards the building. I hauled the unconscious soldier upright and dragged him back to the tank. By the time I had him propped up against one of the tracks, Gurt was on his way back and the building was in flames. Gurt had two companions with him; two women wearing nothing but neck yokes and chains. When they reached the dead guards Gurt stopped them for a moment. One of the women pointed to my captive. I guessed what was required and rifled his pockets. By the time Gurt and the two women reached me I had the key to the yokes. Gurt set about freeing these slaves. I left him to it and methodically slapped my captive to consciousness. Finally I got his attention.

"Now," I said, remembering conversations I'd had like this before, "if you want to live you'll answer my questions. Now, which of the families is providing your lot with weapons?"

"I don't know," he said.

I believed him. He looked scared enough.

"Okay, who will know?"

"I don't know," he said again, sticking to a trusted formula. This time I knew he was lying. Some people just can't help looking shifty when they do it. I reached down and took hold of his hand.

"I'll ask you again, and each time you say 'I don't know' I'll break one of your fingers. It's a tedious process but it always gets results."

"The Bishop knows and the upper Clergy. Soldiers are not told," he said quickly.

That figured.

"Where will I find the Bishop or members of the upper Clergy?"

"In Christoford," he said.

"How do I get . . . no, I think I'll bring you along. You can give me directions."

I hauled him to his feet then looked round at Gurt and the two women.

"What about them?" I asked.

Gurt shrugged.

One of them, a Masai beauty with coal-black skin, looked at me very directly.

"You don't need him." She pointed at the soldier and there was contempt in her expression. "We can lead you there."

"Very well," I said.

I didn't mind. There was seating in the tank for twenty people and room for a lot more. Still holding onto my captive I turned to the tank, then turned back when one of the two women ran back to the dead soldiers and collected their weapons and ammo. Gurt looked on and nodded his approval.

"Please, don't kill me," said the soldier. I had almost forgotten I was holding on to him. I released him and he staggered away. He looked at all of us and began backing off. Gurt started to reach for his pistol but desisted when I looked at him and shook my head. He looked puzzled until I directed his attention to the Masai woman. She had dropped all of her load but for one optek. The soldier turned and ran for the scrub. The optek stuttered out half its thirty-round box. The soldier went head-first into the bushes with one arm and half his back blown away. I climbed onto one of the tank's treads and stepped inside. Gurt followed.

The women's reaction was one of awe. All the screens were on so to them it must have appeared as if the bulkheads and ceilings had disappeared as soon as they got inside. The Masai woman gave me that direct look again.

"Who are you?" she asked.

"The Collector," I told her.

She burst out laughing, but her Asiatic companion seemed not to find the situation so amusing.

"And your names?" I asked.

"I am Bella," said the Masai.

"Vinber," said her companion. Both these women were beautiful. It did not take much thought to figure out their function at the guard post.

"Pleased to meet you. My companion is Gurt. Say hello, Gurt."

Gurt grinned at them with his spiky teeth. Neither of them showed adverse reaction to that. I supposed that they had seen worse things recently. I suspected Gurt now had an addition to his agenda of killing God soldiers and filling his stomach. I directed Bella to the first seat behind Gurt, who was back in the driver's seat. I took my position at the weapons console and kept an eye on the detectors. Vinber sat in one of the many rear seats, with the weapons piled beside her. She was attempting to conceal her nakedness with her hands. I pointed to one of the side lockers.

"You'll find an overall in there," I said, then to Bella, "Where do we go?"

Bella pointed down the track.

"You just follow this for now," she said.

"Is there a more direct route?" I asked.

"Only through the scrub and across the river," she said.

"What direction?"

She pointed. "South east," she said.

How was it, I wondered, that people always seemed to know what direction to go? Until she had pointed I'd thought the south-east behind us.

"Get us going," I said to Gurt.

With another grin Gurt rolled the tank forwards until it was atop the dead soldiers, there he turned it so that like a giant bootheel it ground them into the dirt, then he headed it off into the scrubland. While he was about this I set up a program to run the antipersonnel guns. It was a nasty program, but I thought it appropriate.

By the middle of the night the two women were asleep and Gurt got so weary he knocked over a baobab at least two centuries old and nearly succeeded in tipping us over. No mean feat for a vehicle weighing upwards of thirty tonnes. I called a halt after that and left the three of them bedded down while I went outside and sat on the missile launcher. I sleep occasionally, but it's more psychological thing than a physiological one. I sat on the launcher feeling only a slight need for sleep as I reviewed my long memories. I thought about the two women inside and how they certainly weren't the standard type. When I first came to Africa, fleeing the ice along with many other Europeans, there had been a huge diversity of races on the continent. Over the ensuing centuries those races had mixed in the melting pot of song and the result was those chocolate coloured people by the score. Sometimes there were throwbacks and they were often considered beautiful in their uniqueness. Bella looked pure Masai, and Vinber had the look of a Japanese. Gurt, of course, was something entirely unique and not entirely human. Later, I listened to them inside; to Gurt's gruntings and the moans of the women as he had them one after the other, and wondered what would be the result of this mating. I then closed my eyes and switched my mind to rest mode for a couple of hours.

When I woke, the three of them were soundly asleep. I entered the tank and crept past them to the driving seat. Gurt woke momentarily, watched me, then went back to sleep, the women snuggled in each side of him. I shut off sound to the outside and kept the tank rolling on through the scrub. I was heading

down-slope towards a river and the sun was rising above a stand
of cycads to my left by the time the three woke.

"How far?" I asked Bella, as she stood behind me stretching.

"About twenty kilometres beyond the river," she said, then
went to get a share of the food Gurt was unpacking.

I brought the tank to the edge of the river then ran us in.
There was a sucking sound as all the seals automatically closed.
Soon we were surrounded by a muddy aquarium.

"Jesu!" said Vinber.

Huge perch nosed the tank's armour and a single crocodile
sculled across above us. The tank rolled on and sank deeper and
deeper into mud until we were completely submerged in it. I
only knew we were on our way out when the tank tilted up at
forty-five degrees and began to climb. In a couple of minutes we
were out of mud and fingerlings swarmed about us gobbling up
the creatures we'd uprooted. I brought the tank out of the river
through reed beds. Great clumps of tangled reeds and mud
clung to the tank, and a huge constrictor slid off the back of of
it, evidently bewildered. The mud and reeds were soon scraped
away when I took us straight through a bamboo thicket into an
area scattered with flowering groundsels and the jewelled glitter
of sun birds, then back into acacia scrub. Here I drew the tank to
a halt and bade Gurt to take over. It was only minutes after he
had taken over that we came out of the scrub and went through
a fence into a corn field.

"That is where they kept me," said Bella, pointing to a stockade directly ahead of us. I noted the guard towers and the glint
of sunlight on silver helmets. Beside the stockade was a scattering of barrack buildings. I doubted that any of the Clergy I
wanted would be here and for a moment considered telling Gurt
to go round it, then bullets began to ping off the armour and my
three companions looked at me expectantly. What the hell.

"Take us into that barracks area and stop," I said. While Gurt
did this I initiated the program I'd sorted out earlier.

At one time the problem with automatic guns had been that
they automatically shot anyone. Weapons manufacturers over-
came this by using increasingly sophisticated recognition programs so the guns could identify friends and not shoot them.
Obviously there were problems with this when foes dressed up
as friends, but then any common soldier faced the same problems. The weapons computer I used was the latest development
and could be programmed to the recognise all sort of subtle nu-

ances. In this case I had no need to be subtle. Earlier I'd taken an image of one of the mirrored helmets these God soldiers wore and fed it into the program. As soon as I ran the program the guns simply searched for and shot anyone wearing those helmets.

Gurt took the tank straight through a barracks building, demolishing it and flattening a couple of soldiers who had been a bit tardy of rising. He stopped the tank in the middle of the barracks area then turned to me.

"We kill them now?" he asked. He always seemed to lapse back into this mode of speech when he was excited. I held up my hand.

"It'll start any moment now," I said.

With all the screens on, we had a perfect view. The autoguns appeared as if in thin air above us, turned, fired; single shots, occasional burst of fire. At their elevation I wondered for a moment what they were shooting at, that is until a long burst of fire disintegrated a guard tower and two silver-helmeted corpses fell to the ground. To the right someone fired from a window. It was not until his helmet momentarily showed that the right autogun swivelled and shot him through the wooden wall. Two soldiers ran between buildings firing their opteks on full automatic. One short burst cut them in half. Another soldier ran out with some sort of grenade and never got to throw it. It blew up in what remained of his body. And so it went. I saw a group of four soldiers running through the corn. The guns let them go, as they were without helmets. It took about half an hour before the remaining soldiers got the idea and ran for it. Those without helmets made it. Those with, did not.

When there was no return fire and the autoguns were lazily putting extra bullets in the bloody helmets scattered on the ground, I shut off the program.

"Time to go and liberate some people, I guess," I said, and looked at Gurt. He turned the tank around and drove it towards the stockade. I called up the laser in the carousel and had it log the gate. Gurt drove the tank in over the pile of wood and brought it to a halt.

The more I found out about this Army of God, the more I found a total lack of regret for my actions. There were about a hundred slaves yoked and chained around the edge of the stockade. Some of them were fly-blown corpses, the others skeletally thin but still alive. In the centre of the stockade was the remains of a fire over which had been suspended a cylindrical steel cage. Someone's charred remains clung to the bars. Gurt was first out through the hatch, Bella and Vinber shortly after him. I sat looking at the cage and considered my options. In a moment I decided I would do more than just find out which family had armed these people and attacked me. When I followed the others out of the tank to free the slaves, I approached Bella.

"How many of these stockades are there?" I asked.

"There are many," she replied.

The free men collected weapons, though on my instruction they left the few undamaged helmets where they found them. I searched the barracks until I found a room something like an office. In there I found a map of Cuberland. It wasn't a big place. There were about eight villages scattered around the central town of Christoford. I betted, correctly as it happens, that each of those villages would have a slave stockade. The free men went with their weapons into the fields and the other three rejoined me in the tank while I studied the map.

"Head East, and when you hit a river valley, follow it North," I told Gurt.

"That's not the way to Christoford," said Bella.

"I'm aware of that," I replied. It was five days later, with the tank standing in the wreckage of the eighth stockade, and some five hundred free men camped on the slopes below, when I told Gurt to take us in to Christoford.

Christoford was a sprawling settlement in another of those river valleys. As we came onto the slope above it there was an immediate flash of purple in the night and the tank's ionic shield went up to absorb APW fire. I had Gurt reverse us at high speed back into the thick jungle we had just come through.

"Thought so," I said, then to Gurt and Bella—Vinber had long since abandoned us and joined the other freed slaves—"I want a member of the upper Clergy or the Bishop himself, alive. Can you do that for me?"

"Certainly, Collector," said Bella.

"Course," said Gurt.

"No mistakes. It's going to get bloody down there."

Bella and Gurt took an APW each and quickly got out of the tank. In the jungle all around, my army awaited instructions from General Gurt. I was the first strike. I got into the driving seat and slaved the weapons console to the one before me. First I got the autogun program running, then I got going.

APW fire hit as soon as I came out of the jungle. The shield kept going up on auto and the power drain slowed the tank each time. On the targeting screen I selected anything that looked like a barracks and fired off missiles. Slaves would be killed by this action, but there was no way of avoiding this; war is never clean. The APW fire ceased on about the third missile. The autogun opened up as soon as I hit the main drag and God Soldiers came out shooting. Ahead of me an armoured car swerved round the corner and someone opened up with a belt-fed machine gun. None of the soldiers in the car were wearing the mirrored helms, rather they wore uniform caps. I napalmed them, and while they screamed and burned I rode my tank straight over the car, crushing it completely. After that there were two more armoured cars to which I did the same, then I came to a compound where row upon row of them were parked. Here then was just the place to use the main weapon. I swung the turret, with its two pulsed-energy cannons, round and opened up on the rows of vehicles. The huge injection of energy vaporised metal and caused fuel tanks to explode instantaneously. The armoured fire-filled shells of the cars leapt into the air one after another. Others blew completely apart. Just one strafing rendered them all useless. If they weren't completely wrecked they were buried in wreckage.

Small arms fire, which had been impacting on my tank up to that point, suddenly ceased. I guess a lot of soldiers suddenly realised the futility of what they were doing, and that whatever cover they had was not enough. I halted the tank there before the burning cars and let the U-charger catch up. By now Gurt was leading his small army in to mop up anything I'd left behind. While I waited, APW fire hit my tank again. I traced the source and released a missile in that direction. A three storey concrete building fell into ruin. Something exploded against the side of the tank and I traced the source of that to another concrete building. On the roof two soldiers were operating some sort of grenade launcher. I selected a flack gun from the carousel and dropped a shell on that roof. The shell exploded to release a hundred miniature flack bombs. This had the effect of covering the roof with small explosions and thousands of needle-sized flinders of metal. The men and their launcher disappeared in a haze of red and flame. When things were a bit quieter

I concentrated my attention on the detectors. There was still no sign of any family gun ships, and I guessed that whichever family was involved had considered it prudent to keep their heads down for the present.

By the time I was satisfied with the charge in the batteries there were the sounds of gunfire and explosions from the rear. I moved on, taking streets at random, blowing barracks buildings and killing anyone I discovered in uniform. Any time I started to feel sympathy I remembered the list of punishments I had found in the soldier's pack at the beginning of all this. I remembered those impaled down the sides of the roads, and the burnt corpse clinging to the side of that cylindrical steel cage. It was at the cathedral that I saw the first of the Clergy. They wore robes and tricorn hats and they ran and hid as soon as they could.

The cathedral, as it had been called, was more the size of a medieval church. Wooden frameworks had been erected as a support and guide for mortared blocks of stone. There were no people here, but to one side there was a large slave stockade. I napalmed the building then drove straight at the gate to the stockade. My autoguns took out the soldiers in the two watch towers, then turned their attention to a whole troop of God Soldiers who were attacking from behind. I knocked the gate flat and drove on top of it. There must have been two hundred slaves in there, all of them chained and yoked. My autoguns where now spitting only the occasional shot. Behind were the bodies of about a hundred God Soldiers strewn across the street. Five thousand of them, that first soldier had told me. I wondered how many I had accounted for and how many were running. I drove on into the stockade and with the laser I targeted the wall mounts for the chains. After I'd hit about three, the slaves got the idea and started feeding the chains through the loops on their yokes. Once I'd hit every mount I got out of my seat and got out of my tank.

The slaves stood their ground as I approached. They started to back up when I drew my QC laser. I stepped in and grabbed the nearest one by his yoke.

"Keep still, idiot. I'm freeing you," I said as he struggled.

He did as I said and I inspected the locking mechanism of the yoke. A short burst from the laser cut through a forged bar and the yoke fell open.

"Thank you, master," said the man.

"I'm not a master," I said, handing him the laser. "Free your fellows. There's weapons out there you can use if you wish. Or you can get out of here. Don't put on their helmets."

He looked puzzled and it was convenient that a God soldier chose that moment for suicidal attack. He ran into the compound yelling and firing his optek. He hit about three slaves and was coming at me before one of the autoguns tracked and fired. One shot, cleanly through his helmet. He went down like a brick.

"Leave their helmets alone," I said, pointing at the soldier's helmet. Blood was pulsing out of the entry hole. The exit hole was a torn mess out of which brains and skull fragments had flowered. I returned to my tank.

It was a long night. By dawn the fighting was over and the looting and celebrations begun. Many of those celebrations involved doing unspeakable things to the captives. I guess cruelty is catching. Some of the slaves found a store of stakes, and soldiers were soon decorating every street corner, either on stakes or dangling over fires. As I sat in my tank in the ruins of the small cathedral, awaiting Gurt's arrival, I saw one of the Clergy dragged screaming out of a building. They stripped him and hung him upside down, split him open and slowly pulled his intestines out. His wife and his two children they were kinder to. They only raped her a couple of times in front of the children before beating the three of them to death with the butts of their opteks.

Gurt arrived with an escort of ten freed slaves to keep others from taking his captive. Other slaves followed, yelling and threatening. One woman ran at the black-clad figure with a carving knife in her hand. Gurt casually took the knife out of her hand and shoved her back into her fellows. I climbed out of my tank and walked to meet them. When I got there, Gurt had the bound captive brought forward and thrown at my feet. It was all very dramatic.

"Bishop," he said.

"Give him to us!" yelled someone in the crowd, and that yell was taken up by others. No one had used an optek against one of their fellows yet, but it looked likely to happen. There was much jostling and people began to push forwards. I did my little trick with my face and the jostling at the front of the crowd stopped.

"He is mine!" I shouted, and some bastard shot me.

The bullets of course had no effect other than to put holes in my outer covering and ricochet away. When I stood there looking at them with my ceramal face, unaffected by the round I had taken in my chest, the crowd got a little quieter. Someone said, "Oh shit." I put my face back on, reached down and hauled the Bishop to his feet. He'd been badly beaten and seemed not to know what was going on. I looked at Gurt.

"You coming?" I asked.

He nodded. I tucked my captive under my arm, leapt up onto the tread of my tank and went inside. He followed. When I later asked him what had happened to the two women I discovered that they had fled on discovering his eating habits.

The Bishop was a diminutive little man of about sixty years. His face was brown and wrinkled and he only had a few scraps of white hair on his head. At some time in his past he had lost an eye and the socket was filled with a glass eye of the wrong colour. During the journey back to my cave he remained sullenly silent, his gaze fixed firmly on the floor. When we arrived and after I shut down the tank, I turned to him.

"What's your name?" I asked him.

He looked up at me with his good eye wide open.

"I am Dextroth the one true vicar of Christos the one true God," he said, perhaps expecting me to be impressed.

"Where did you get your weapons, Dextroth?"

"The one true Drowned God provides," he said.

In retrospect I wished Gurt had grabbed one of the Upper Clergy rather than this individual. I doubted I'd get much sense out of him.

"Who were the Drowned God's agents in this case then?" I asked.

"This information is the privilege only of the one true God's Vicar and his Clergy," he said. It seemed to me that he was incapable of saying any sentence without injecting a 'one true' into it.

"Skin him?" Gurt suggested.

I thought not. I'd seen his type before amongst the Sheta-protestanti. It wouldn't have surprised me had he been a member of that group at some time in his past.

"No, bring him," I said.

We exited the tank and I led the way to a stair from the cave. This took us up to a steel door which would only open for me.

Beyond the door was one of the laboratories I used for research, repairs, all sorts of things. I had Gurt tie Dextroth to a chair then I checked through storage compartments until I found what I wanted. It took about an hour to get through the bullshit, but the scopolamine derivatives did the trick. I got the name I wanted and this caused me some amusement. By way of the river-cave door we went to the wing. I let Gurt have his way with the old man there and we left what remained of him with the rest of the cockroaches.

Once back at the complex I immediately checked to see which of the shuttles was ready to go into orbit. A huge flying-wing heavy lifter was due to leave in one hour. I hurried to find Susan and soon learned that she was up on the main JMCC station. With Gurt I went up to her office, and while Gurt fed himself I had a conversation with Molly.

"How does my JMCC stock stand at present?" I asked.

"You are still the primary shareholder with fifty-eight percent of the stock," the AI replied.

"Okay, but I gave Jethro Susan powers to act on my behalf. What have been her main moves over the last few months?"

"Jethro Susan has increased JMCC mining interests in the asteroidal belt."

"And that's mainly Enmark territory isn't it?" I said.

The AI emulation of my long-dead friend confirmed this for me.

"If I died, Jethro Susan would receive most of my stock and immediately assume cardinal status. What would happen if she died as well?"

"The stock would go on the open market and Fearson would assume the directorship."

"How does Fearson stand on the increased mining activities?"

"He is against them. His preference is for further development of JMCC banking and stockbroking."

"So if he assumed the directorship the mining development would be scrapped."

"This is most likely."

I thought about that. It was the Enmarks who had supplied weapons to the Army of God. They probably intended to shove JMCC out to the belt by killing off myself and Susan, thus promoting this Fearson to the Directorship. This did not prove that Fearson was necessarily guilty of anything, though I suspected he probably was. All that remained for me to figure out was what purpose the Enmarks had for Gurt's kind. If, indeed, it was the Enmarks who had created the sauramen. I was beginning to have my doubts. Did the Enmarks plan all-out war? It was time to nip things in the bud.

"Molly, I want you to direct link me to the Enmark AI," I said.

It took a minute or so, then a completely different voice spoke to me. This was the gruff and irritated voice of a man.

"Enmark AI online," he said. "What is the purpose of this communication?"

"Hello, David, it is the Collector here. Look under file code ABG413," I said.

Most of the major family AIs are downloaded mind recordings of important humans who died long ago. Molly Canard I had put in charge of JMCC a thousand years ago. It had been her idea to have a memplant installed. When she died at the ripe old age of two hundred and five I'd downloaded her memcording into the JMCC system. Her psychological status had made it impossible for her to be like me. She would have self-destructed after only a few years. In the JMCC system it was possible to change her program and remove those self-destructive aspects of her character. David Enmark had been a different case altogether.

Eight centuries ago David had been one of JMCC's best mining engineers, but far too fiercely independent to fit in well. I'd liked him; his attitude had been much like mine. When he tried to form a breakaway cooperative, rather than shoot him down in flames I financed him and let him get on with it. The solar system is big. There's room for everyone . . . or there was then. He formed his little company shortly after Molly was downloaded into the JMCC system. Immortality attracted him and he decided to get himself a memplant. He built his mining cooperative into a huge corporation over the next century and when he died during a risky mercury-mining expedition—he'd always liked to keep his hand in—he was downloaded into the Enmark system. Because of my initial financing of his operation I retained a large proportion of Enmark stock. The details of this were kept in archive file ABG413 and I had never until now used the power that controlling interest gave me.

"You bastard," said David Enmark.

"Yes," I said, "and a bastard with cardinal status. Who's Director there now?"

"Callum Manx Enmark. He's distantly related and a canny bugger," David replied.

"I take it that he's taken exception to JMCC interests in the belt?"

"Yes."

"He had the Army of God supplied with weapons and the instruction to kill me?"

"Yes."

"What about Jethro Susan?"

"That's Alex Fearson's job."

"I see. What can you tell me about the project in Madagascar?"

"The sauramen are a recent discovery. It is posited that they are the private project of JMCC or the Jupiter Bank," he said reluctantly. The Jupiter Bank; a Corporation but not a corporate family. The people and AIs that ran it usually kept in the background making pots of money out of other people's disputes and deals.

"Go on," I said. He didn't want to answer me, but he was the Enmark AI and I had the controlling interest, so he was incapable of not answering.

"Callum believes the sauramen are the fodder for someone else's private army. An army formed as a counter to his steadily growing Army of God. His God soldiers he plans to use as storm troopers to take the other family stations. He has training stations and an assault craft manufactory in the belt."

The reply was terse but it provided me with much of the information I required.

"Very well. I now assume the Directorship of the Enmark Corporation. Tell this Callum to stand down and await my arrival. Also give the order that all operations in the belt are to cease immediately," I said.

"Issuing order now. You are—"

David's voice was cut off with a buzz of static.

"Molly, what happened?"

"There was an explosion aboard the Enmark station. Their system is now offline."

"Shit . . . Put me in contact with Jethro Susan."

"She has been monitoring."

"Susan?"

"I heard you," replied my wife, and there was a flickering in the middle of the room. Her projected hologram appeared hovering a few centimetres above the floor.

"You'll deal with Fearson?" I asked her.

Rather than reply she reached forward and adjusted the feed from her holocamera. The hologram expanded across the carpet to show a hovering corpse with its neck twisted out of place. Jank stood over this corpse, his wig and cosmetic work mussed to expose the scales on his head and face.

"Fearson?" I asked.

She nodded in reply.

"And I see Jank appears rather familiar," I said.

She shrugged.

So, Jethro Susan was responsible for the sauramen.

"When did you find out about Enmark's plans?" I asked.

"Not until now. We knew one of the Families was supplying a fanatical group on Earth and building up their numbers. It's been going on for seventy years. We couldn't find out who was responsible so we started the Madagascan project as a counter to it. That was fifty years ago," she replied.

"We?" I asked.

"The Jupiter Bank."

"I see." I looked at Gurt, who seemed to be concentrating on his food. I wasn't fooled. He was taking all of this in. I thought about what she and the Bank had done. It occurred to me that for an Army of God whose beliefs did not encompass such Godless things as evolution, the perfect enemies would be people whose ancestry could be directly traced to the dinosaurs. This was also the kind of irony that Susan loved.

"What about what happened to Gurt?" I asked.

"The Enmarks and other Families found out about his kind shortly after we instituted the project. We pulled out and left it. It could have caused major problems. Other Families have snatched sauramen since then to study. I would say the Enmarks started it recently with a view to recruiting."

"A complete turnaround then," I said.

"The sauramen and the army aren't really the problem anymore. The Enmark station's the big problem. If I'd have known you were a majority stockholder we could perhaps have prevented a deal of grief," she said.

"Perhaps," I said. I had always kept my cards close to my chest and I saw no reason to change even then. Again, I looked at

Gurt, who was sitting at her desk calmly feeding chicken legs into his mouth. I couldn't read his expression.

"I'll deal with the station," I said. "Molly, order that heavy lifter unloaded of its present cargo, then load a hundred and fifty skirmish guns with two hundred rounds each." Then I turned back to Susan, who had yet to cut her hologram.

"Where did you get the DNA?" I asked.

"There's been a working template for sauraman DNA in the system since JMCC was founded. It was one of their initial projects," she replied.

"Ah," I said, brilliantly. I was the founder of JMCC and I didn't know about it. Well, I guess you can be a super-being and not know everything.

The pilot and navigator of the heavy lifter were a little dubious of my instructions.

"A water landing?" the pilot asked.

"You can handle it?" I asked in return.

"I can handle it," he said, and returned to the controls.

Below us Madagascar was spread in all shades of green in the azure of the Indian ocean. I don't know what it was called now, but the lake that soon came into view below us had once been called Lake Itasy. Gurt told me it was in the thick jungles around this lake that most of his people lived. While the pilot brought us down I walked back into the huge hold which extended into the thick wings of the heavy lifter. The cargo I had ordered put aboard occupied one small corner. Gurt had one of the crates open and was inspecting the weapons inside. The problem with fighting a battle on a station is that high velocity weapons will punch through the hull to the detriment of friend and foe alike. In these cases were guns that fired mercury shot. Each took a fifty round box and could fire on automatic. The mercury shot would kill a man, unless armoured, but not puncture hull metal.

"Think they'll be able to handle them?" I asked Gurt.

"We're not complete primitives," he replied.

I let that go then decided to be direct.

"You heard Jethro Susan. Do you still want to kill God soldiers?"

"They killed Horl and the rest," he said.

"That's not what I'm getting at," I said.

"My mother's mother remembers the teachers. No-one believes the first comers, but now I see it is true," he said, and it took me a moment to figure out.

"Jethro Susan and JMCC," I said.

He nodded.

"Do you hate them?" I asked.

"How can I hate what created me?" he asked, and that, I guess, was that.

The pilot brought the lifter down on the glittering waves of the lake, adjusted AG to keep it buoyant, then with delicate touches on the thrusters had it drifting to the shore. It hit a floating mass of lily pads before the shore, but on AG he got us over them and finally up against a vine-covered slope below thick jungle. I went to the main-bay door as it opened down to make a ramp to the slope. When the door was finally down I made to step out on the ramp. Four heavy arrows thumped into my chest. I guessed the natives were unfriendly.

About forty of them came roaring out of the jungle armed with bows, wide-bladed spears, one or two opteks, and what looked like muzzle-loaders. Their charge stuttered to a halt when they saw me still standing at the ramp pulling the arrows out of myself and discarding them. Gurt stepped to my side then and babbled something at them that was a mishmash of Urtak-Swahili, and Old French and Portuguese. I was impressed. It seemed to me that this meant his standard Family English had been recently acquired.

A large saurawoman—I later discovered that the women were all bigger and more ornery than the men—walked to the head of the crowd and burbled back at him. It took a moment or two for my autotranslator to get up to speed. When it did, I replayed the conversation and followed it through:

"Who are you who comes with this armoured meat?" she asked.

"I am Gurt of the Ankatra. Lieutenant of Horl Lord of Ankatra," he said.

"And I'm a lemur."

"I am Gurt and I will prove this on your flesh if you doubt," said Gurt.

After this friendly exchange the female looked to one of her fellows.

"He's Gurt," said that one.

"What do you want, Gurt?" she asked.

"Is there no courtesy here?" Gurt asked.

The saurawoman, whom I later learned to be called Sophist—an interesting name—reluctantly welcomed us and invited
us to her village. Before going with Gurt I instructed the pilot to
close up the lifter and stay alert. Sophist led us down a jungle
trail, all her fighters gathered close around us. I expected to
come into a village of wattle huts with streets smelling of sewer-
age. The village was nothing like that. It was very much like a
Cotswold hamlet transported into the middle of a jungle. It was
tidy. The stone houses had neatly tended gardens and multicol-
oured vines growing up the walls. Sophist led us to a communal
eating hall, with tables and chairs of fine-grained wood neatly
set out in rows. The one fly in this particular pot of ointment
was the gutted human corpse roasting on a spit over an open fire
at the end of the room. As we entered the room I felt someone
prodding at my leg and looked down at a naked child of the village. The little boy was more heavily scaled than the adults and
he had a long tail. I guessed part of the growing up process for
him was the losing of that tail.

"Not food," one of the adults told that child and he scam-
pered away.

Soon after we had entered the hall other villagers began to file
in. Gurt leapt up onto a table and stood there waiting until everyone was in. I ended up with armed adults crammed all
around me, all of them looking at me speculatively. They turned
their attention from me when Gurt began to speak.

"I am Gurt, lieutenant to Horl of Ankatra. Horl of Ankatra
is now dead," he said, eliciting much muttered disbelief. Gurt
continued, "The child stealers came to Ankatra and we fought
them as we always do. This time they had not come for our children. They took Horl and myself and seven brave fighters of the
Mark. They took us up." Gurt pointed at the ceiling then went
on to tell them all he had told me. He told them of his meeting
with me and those speculative gazes were fixed on me again.

"He is meat," said a sauraman standing right next to me.

"He is not. He is the Collector of legend. He is the man machine," said Gurt.

This was the first I'd heard of Gurt's knowledge of me. His
people must have either picked it up from the JMCC 'teachers'
or from the people they fed upon when not arguing about 'lemu
rights'.

"Meat," said the arguer, prodding me with one horny claw.

"Show them, Collector," said Gurt.

I was getting tired of pulling my face off so I turned to the arguer. He held at his side a muzzle-loader with a long and heavy steel barrel. I took it off him. He tried to resist and a look of surprise appeared on his face when he found he could not. When he released his weapon I bent the barrel in half then handed it back to him.

"Strong meat," said someone, and there was a general tittering.

"The child stealers live in a great building high in the sky. They are our enemies and they are enemies of the Collector. We go there to do battle with them. Who will come?"

There was no sudden rush of volunteers.

"We will consider what you have said," said Sophist. "Now you must eat with us."

I sat at the table with the arguer on my left and Gurt on my right. Sophist sat opposite us. I refused the meat, but not the drink made from fermented lilies that was passed around. Sophist got the prime cut of the meat, which to these people was the head. She broke it open and scooped out steaming brains with a clam shell. The next course was the crackling, nice and salty, and passed down the tables on trays. Next came slices of meat in deep bowls. Sauraman children ran about munching on nicely crisped hands and feet. Large pots were then brought out in which whole lemurs had been boiled with some sort of greenery. The roast human had obviously only been a starter. I asked Gurt about this and he said it was because of their rarity now.

"Do your people build sailing ships?" I asked him.

"Yes," said Gurt, and grinned at me.

I visualised the future of Earth humans when the Madagascan sauraman population overflowed onto mainland Africa. It looked bleak for them.

We returned to the lifter at nightfall, after receiving Sophist's promise that the news and the request Gurt had brought would be disseminated amongst the other villages. Gurt slept a contented sleep that night in the cargo area. The pilot and navigator banned him from the fore-section sleeping area because of the sudden stinking flatulence he suffered.

"What the hell has he been eating?" the pilot asked.

I thought it best not to tell him.

During the night I watched as sauramen and women gathered on the shore and lit campfires there. By dawn there were about forty of them, and when Gurt finally woke and went to greet them, there were twenty more. He took with him a few of the weapons we had brought and the recruits had a high old time blasting away at the trees and anything foolish enough to show itself in the upper branches. By midday there were over a hundred sauramen and women, which was getting towards the full load the lifter could manage. I instructed the pilot to keep the door between the fore section and the cargo bay closed unless I requested it be opened. Then told Gurt to bring our recruits aboard.

Space stations are, by their nature, normally impossible to attack unless by subterfuge. Computer-controlled shield projectors, lasers, missiles, and pulsed-energy cannons, would be enough to deal with any attack. There was the possibility that a ship the size of a station, carrying the same armament and shielding, might be able to do the job, just as a fleet of ships might be able to, though not without huge damages and losses. The Enmark station was one of the smaller ones, at only a kilometre in diameter and two long. It supported a population of ten thousand or more. It might have seemed madness to try to board it with only a hundred or so sauramen, but for a few critical factors.

Callum Manx Enmark was no longer the Director and no longer had cardinal status. In an attempt to retain power he had obviously blown the computer system. This meant that all computer-controlled shields and weapons were out; we should be able to board. There might be fire from manually operated weapons, but I was sure the lifter's own defences would deal with them adequately. Once on board I reckoned on us facing resistance from people personally loyal to Callum, not from the entire ten thousand. Most of the people on the station were civilians and would be keeping their heads down until things were resolved. Callum's actions, by corporate law, were illegal, and some of those civilians might even be on my side. All I intended was for the sauramen to get me through so I could kick Callum out of office and put the system back online. I didn't expect a lot of resistance.

As the lifter cruised towards the station and adjusted its attitude for docking, I stayed alert at the weapon's console. There was no attack at all as we closed in and none while we docked.

This puzzled me. I'd at least expected a couple of missiles to be fired at the lifter. Nothing.

Docking clamps crashed into position and the lifter was set against the station like a fly come to suck blood. I went back into the hold where the sauramen waited. They sat on the floor all armed with nice new weapons, complemented by the occasional spear or muzzle-loader. With Gurt's and Sophist's help I manually engaged the airlock and we were ready to go in.

"You'll find the floor here a little unnerving. The gravity of the ship is at ninety degrees to that of the station. The corridor here will appear to curve down to a precipice. That precipice is the floor of the bay area," Gurt looked puzzled. "Just follow me," I said.

I led them to the down-curving corridor. Halfway round, with my body at an attitude of forty-five degrees to them, I looked back.

"Come on," I said.

Gurt was the first to follow; tentatively, as if someone was going to snatch the floor from underneath him. The rest of them held back until they saw him walking, without ill effect, around the curve. Soon all of us were coming out into the open bay area. The first shots were fired then, and when I saw their source I knew we were in trouble.

The soldiers ran out of the back of the bay, armed with slow pulse guns. These were another weapon designed to kill on-station without penetrating the hull. They fired disperse pulses of ions that electrocuted those they hit. The men carrying these weapons wore black uniforms and mirrored helmets. The Army of God was here and there would be more resistance than I had expected.

Sophist was the first to be hit by the bluish haze of an ion bolt. She convulsed where she stood while small lightnings earthed themselves from her to the floor. The sauramen opened fire with their weapons and two soldiers disintegrated where they stood. Then everyone was running for cover and blasting away as they did so. I dropped to one knee where I was and opened up on full automatic, emptying box after box at the charging soldiers, forcing them quickly into cover so all the sauramen could get out of the ship. I used the same weapon as my sauramen, not the APW I had strapped across my back; that was for later, when we were deeper into the station. Four ion bolts hit me while I was there and I was paralysed while each discharged into the floor. Once the last had discharged I started firing again and ran for cover myself. All the sauramen were in the bay now, and I was getting double vision and some strange error messages from my system monitors.

The battle from then on seemed to be all firing without very many people getting hit. The ion bolts discharged through the crates, autohandlers and small transports the sauramen hid behind, whilst the mercury shot they fired was easily stopped by the same. No one seemed to be inclined to heroism. Everyone wanted to stay alive. The fight could not continue like this though. We had limited ammunition and the soldiers probably did not. We had limited numbers yet these soldiers could be reinforced at any time. I guessed that they were the nearest to the bay at which we docked, and that there would be others scattered all over the station. I decided it was time for me to act. About ten metres from where I crouched was an autohandler with grab arms and heavy forklift. Most of the soldiers were crouched behind a row of packing cases, some blasted open to expose the rough aluminium castings inside. The handler was just the job.

I ran across the intervening area and leapt up behind the panel through which the handler could be programmed. Feeling a touch of deja vu I reached under the panel and tore away a bunch of optic cables. Two ionic bolts hit me one after the other as I got hold of the panel, twisted it, and tore it away. Underneath the panel I exposed the original manual controls and the servo motors that operated them. I pulled the servo motors free. Another bolt hit me and lines ran down my vision and there was a weird whistling in my ears. Using the manual controls I turned the handler and had it pick up the nearest convenient crate. With this positioned before me to absorb the bolts I looked around at the crouching sauramen.

"Charge!" I yelled, feeling slightly strange.

Sauramen fell in behind the handler as I drove it at the line of crates. The handler went through the line with a crash and the sauramen leapt up onto the scattered crates and fired down at the soldiers. I leapt from my seat, up onto the crate the handler had suspended three metres in the air, and opened fire from there. Another ionic bolt hit me and caused random squares to appear in my vision and the ringing in my ears turned to a steady thumping. I saw that the shot had come from across the bay area, and that it was shots from there that were also picking off my men. I leapt from the crate and hit the ground running.

At the bottom right of my vision a little red light was flashing. This meant that my autorepair system had been activated. I rounded the small shuttle, from behind which the shots had come, and charged straight into a group of four soldiers. I went into them with my weapon on automatic. They hit me a couple of more times, but to no avail. Their shots just put a few more squares across my vision. It wasn't really fair, but then whoever said life was?

The remaining soldiers retreated down the corridors and escalators from the bay area. There were about forty bodies scattered across the decking. The numbers looked about even, but to my surprise I saw that some of them were stirring; the sauramen. They were tough buggers. After a few minutes, while weapons were collected and bodies checked, about half the sauramen had revived. It turned out that the only ones dead were those that had been struck by three or more ionic bolts. There was a number still unconscious. I had them taken back to the lifter, before calling together the remainder of the sauramen and leading them, down a wide escalator, to a precinct that led into the centre of the station. The precinct was a tubular structure with sky-effect ceiling panels, lawns, gardens and decorative pathways down its centre, and shops and restaurants down the sides. It was deserted and I didn't like it.

"You can bet your life there are autoguns down here somewhere," I said. Gurt nodded in understanding; after being in my tanks he knew about autoguns. Sophist, who was one of those to have recovered, did not know, and Gurt explained to her in low tones. I removed the APW from my back and led them all to one side of the precinct. Before me was a sign advertising 'The Best Synthetastes This Side Of Jupiter'. On the menu was a list that included a 'dinosaur meat selection, trilobite thermador, and human flesh'. I did a double-take at the first and the last on the list.

On a low setting I used the APW to take out the tinted window of the restaurant. The small blast cut a hole the size of a head through the glassite, then as the chain molecules unravelled, the whole window fell as a sheet of dust.

"Come on," I said, leading them in. "We go round."

The restaurant was all hexagonal tables and bucket chairs. As we moved through, a floating vendor shaped like an ancient one-armed bandit came directly towards me.

"Tables for one hundred and three, sir?" it asked, before a broad-bladed spear struck it and set it tumbling through the air trailing wisps of smoke.

"Table bzzzp. Drink bzzzp. Let me clean that up bzzzp," it said, repeatedly as it tumbled. We moved to the back wall of the restaurant.

"This should do," I said, and shifted up the setting on my APW. I didn't know what was behind this wall, though I thought it likely not to be living quarters. With a flash and crash the back wall of the restaurant buckled and blasted away. Beyond it the dust of its disintegration settled on the automachines of a manufactory. Here were the computer-controlled mills, lathes, presses that have been an indispensable part of industry since industry began. The sauramen looked with suspicion at the machines, but there were no thrown spears as in the restaurant. We moved down aisles wide enough for us to walk three abreast, but which had been designed for maintenance and material-loading robots. This was not a place where people would very often come. Anything anyone wanted made would first be constructed, viewed, and tested in a computer in the comfort of someone's apartment or office. The instructions would then come down here by optic cable and the machines would do the work.

The manufactory ended at another main-section wall in which were wide sliding doors and a simple door control. There was no need for me to blow another hole. Beyond these was a huge materials store, with racked bars and ingots of machinable metals, ceramics, plastics, glasses, and a thousand other materials with numbers rather than names. I warned the sauramen to be wary now. We had not gone the way expected, but by now more soldiers would have been moved to intercept us. I was not wrong.

On the treble-click, sauramen were diving for cover amongst the stacks of materials. The twin barrels of the machine gun filled the room with ricocheting flack bullets. Flinders and fragments tore in every direction. Two sauramen had no time to get to cover and simply flew apart. Before a round struck me square in the forehead, and I staggered and fell backwards over a stack of bearing cases, I saw that the twinned guns had been mounted on one of the maintenance robots, and that soldiers were coming in behind it. As I hit the ground I managed one shot before the APW was torn from my hand, its casing smashed. The robot ground to a halt, half its side blasted away. Momentarily the guns were firing at the ceiling, then they swivelled down concentrating their fire on me. They were remotely controlled and whoever was controlling them knew who their greatest danger was. Bearing cases crashed all around me and multiple hits slid me back across the floor. My syntheflesh covering was stripped from my torso and my arms as I tried to rise. I didn't see her do it. I had too many problems of my own at that moment. It was Sophist who leapt up onto a stack of copper ingots and fired an entire box down on the twinned guns. She shut them down, but in repayment was cut in half by optek fire.

In the bloody scramble that followed I realised I had made a big mistake. No one in command on a station would allow soldiers to carry weapons that might penetrate the hull. There would be no APWs or hard rounds, no pulsed-energy weapons or high intensity lasers, but there would be weapons capable of stopping me. I considered pulling out then, but thought it unlikely we would be able to get the lifter away. We had to carry on. I had to use my abilities to their fullest extent.

While the fire-fight continued, I stood then ran to where the soldiers were taking cover. I used no weapon but myself. Optek fire and ionic bolts struck me repeatedly. My autorepair system went wild with error messages. I reached three soldiers crouching behind a rack of metal bars, snatched an optek from one and used it to brain the other two, then picked the other one up and threw him at some of his fellows who had rushed to help. Four men went down in a tangle. I dragged a copper alloy bar from the rack and walking with it held as a staff I advanced on others who had taken cover. The ionic bolts that hit me now mostly discharged down through the bar into the floor. Optek fire put me out of balance as it stripped away my outer covering, but the bullets ricocheted off my ceramal skeleton. After the next group of soldiers I stepped away with the bar bent and running with gore. My sauramen came in after me. The soldiers started to realise then that their weapons had little effect on me and that hiding was no use. I suppose I killed about forty of them in the next ten minutes. I don't like to examine those memories too closely. Suffice to say that soon they were running for their lives, many of them abandoning their weapons.

"Come on!" I yelled to my small army, and they followed. I got some strange looks from them as I tore away fragments of syntheflesh that still clung, to reveal the me underneath. What they saw was a metal skeleton with white teeth and, when my shutters came up, lidless grey eyes. My rib cage is a solid thing in which most of my systems are contained, and my spine a column ten centimetres in diameter.

We charged to the end of the materials store after the retreating soldiers, then I took them away from that course down service corridors and through a hydroponics section. Beyond this there was more resistance in the form of another twinned machine flack gun. I took them away from this to a central point where the drop shafts had been shut down. All around were corridors and maintenance tunnels spreading into many hydroponics sections. Here I decided what I must do and turned to them.

"You've got me this far, and from here I must continue alone. I'll only get more of you killed if I bring you further. Spread out here and hide, or hunt, whatever you wish. This will be over within the hour," I said.

"I come with you," said Gurt.

"You can't," I said.

"I come," he said.

I reached round and grabbed him by the throat. I lifted him off the floor and looked at him, squares fleeing across my vision and error messages flashing up all over the place.

"Where I'm going you won't be able to survive. Stay here and hold. Trust me." With that I dropped him and jumped into the drop shaft. He didn't follow.

For a thousand years many stations used rotation to simulate gravity. On other stations people adapted and were adapted to live without gravity. There is a whole race of humans in the Sol system who remain apart from Earth-normal humans because a meeting could be fatal. These weightless adapted humans have bones as brittle as egg-shell and severely atrophied muscles. When, as a result of the accruing Unification Formulae, came methods of gravity and antigravity generation, many stations received a radical overhaul. The Enmark station was cylindrical and had once spun around its axis. Its floors had been arranged concentrically having a simulated gravity of one and a half gees at the outside and zero at the centre. With the advent of gravity generators, floors had been put in across the cylinder, so in effect it had become a cylindrical tower. Transport from top to bottom of the tower was by drop shafts. In these, irised gravity

fields squirted people in whatever direction they chose. With
the shafts shut down there was no gravity field, just weightless-
ness. I hit the opposing wall of the shaft and, driving the tips of
my metal fingers into a ridge, flung myself upwards. I did this
again and again until I was travelling at about forty kilometres
per hour. Over-spill of gravity generation from each floor
tugged at me slightly as I sped past, but did not slow me much.
With my weight came a lot of inertia. I turned as I hurtled upwards and readied myself. I hit the top of the shaft about a minute later.

The metal boomed under my feet and I left two foot-shaped
dents in it. The rebound had me floating down to the entrance
to the top floor. Upside down in relation to that floor, I looked
through into the corridor beyond. Standing in the centre of the
corridor was a three barrelled machine gun behind which sat a
woman dressed in blue coveralls and mirrored helmet. She must
have been Enmark rather than God soldier. She didn't see me
until I waved at her. I must have gone past too fast.

"Jesu!" she said and opened up with the gun. I suppose it
must be disconcerting to suddenly see an upside down metal
skull grinning at you from the end of the corridor. I hauled myself out of the way until the firing ceased, then stuck my head
down again.

"Missed me!" I shouted. I was feeling a bit flaky after all those
ionic bolts. She opened up again and I could hear her yelling
into a communicator.

"Missed again!"

She ran out of ammunition on the fourth occasion. I stuck
my head round, about a hundred bullets smashed into the back
wall of the shaft, then the gun kept making its repeated treble
clicks as she refused to take her hand off the trigger. I dropped
down through the door to the floor and she sat there behind her
gun pale-faced, waiting for me to come and kill her. I clicked
one eye-shutter down in a metallic wink, turned, squatted down,
then launched myself with my fingers speared, at the back wall
of the shaft. The bullets had done what I required of them. The
metal gave and I punched a hole, which I then tore wider to get
me through. Beyond this I tore through thick insulation to a
second thinner skin of metal. I stabbed my hand through this,
tore a rent, and stepped through.

Beyond the wall was an apartment. A man and a small boy crouched to one side. The man held a console on his lap and had a laser pistol at his side. He looked at me.

"Funny man," said the boy, pointing at me.

"Collector," said the man. I walked over to him, reached down and picked up the pistol. "Cardinal status," he said. I nodded to him and headed for the door. He had locked himself in. I decided it best to leave him that safety.

"Code," I said. He told me, I punched it, and walked out into the corridor.

This upper residential section was separate from where I wanted to go. Here the Director's staff and wealthier stationers resided. I reckoned there would be more defences between me and Callum Manx Enmark. As a last resort I'd no doubt he had loyal soldiers armed with APWs and the like. I bet on him having every access covered with enough armament to blow the top off the station. He was probably suited now and getting ready to board his personal transport. I also bet on him not covering one other option.

I am not a man. I am metal, nano-circuitry, and syntheflesh, though not the latter at that moment. All that is human of me is a brain and spinal column held at absolute zero in a superconducting grid. Because I normally look like a man people make the mistake of expecting me to have a man's requirements. I do not need to eat, nor do I need to breath.

The airlock was at the centre of this residential section. I went through into vacuum on the top of the station, fused the locking mechanism with the laser, then walked across the metal surface towards the centre of the station. There I could see the dome of the Director's apartments and control centre. Next to an extensible airlock was a fast shuttle; a craft shaped like a flattened egg. I walked across to the dome, found a window, and looked inside.

There was much activity in the control centre; people in blue overalls were running about, others in Enmark businesswear were arguing, punching at consoles, and generally looking as if they wished they were somewhere else. I watched this chaos for a moment then moved on to the airlock. Even as I arrived it was being extended to the shuttle. No doubt my presence on the upper floors had been reported and Callum was taking the precaution of getting himself aboard. From there I supposed he could still run things, then run, if it became necessary. I climbed into the extending tube of the lock and hung on.

The tubular corridor hit against the side of the shuttle and locked down. Immediately air rushed in and filled it. I watched frost forming on my hands while I sat on the floor and waited. Eventually the lock was up to pressure and the station door whined and clunked, then opened inwards.

"You can't mean it," a woman said.

"I damned well can. I've spent years on this project and I'm not having some pre-Convulsion 'chronism dictating terms. We blow the top as soon as he's in the control room."

The second voice I recognised as the voice that had spoken to me before my tank was destroyed by the sun laser; Callum Manx Enmark.

"You can't do that," said the woman.

"I won't let you do that," said a third voice, that of a man.

"Leave it," said Callum.

By then the door was halfway open.

"You'll die," said Callum.

The door swung full open on a strange little diarama. A short stocky thug in grey businesswear had his hand poised at his jacket pocket. He was facing me. A ginger-haired woman in a clinging wrap and spring heels stood next to him. With his back to me was a tall man with long curly blond hair. He held a laser pistol, similar to the one I held, on the two of them. The thug saw me and commendably showed little reaction other than a widening of his eyes. The woman saw me and screamed. I pressed the snout of my recently filched laser against the back of Callum's neck.

"Drop it," I said.

He turned and fired.

The laser scored a groove across my rib cage, then flashed beyond me into the airlock. Of a sudden there was the roar of escaping air. The man and woman held themselves in the station lock as it automatically began to close. Callum was pulled off his feet and slammed into me. As I closed my hand on the edge of the lock he hung onto my arm. I looked at him then released my hold and stepped back into the tunnel. The station lock closed. Callum looked at me in horror as his eyes bulged and air jetted from his lungs. The last of the air gusted from the tunnel and he lay on the floor gulping, water vapour puffing from his mouth and swollen eyes. His body swelled as that of a fish

pulled up from deepest sea. It took him about two minutes, I
suppose. I wasn't really counting. I just watched and thought
about the slaves of the Army of God, Sophist and those other
sauramen that had died, and of David Enmark finally sent into
oblivion . . . When it was finished I walked over and knocked
hard on the station airlock. About a quarter of an hour later
they let me in. An hour after that the remaining sauramen were
back on the lifter and certain Enmark activities shut down. I decided that I would stay until the Enmark system was back online
and until I had decided who to put in charge. The irony was that
the only available memplant for the system AI came from a
bloated corpse brought in from outside, and that because I effectively owned the Enmark Corporation, Callum Manx
Enmark would spend the rest of his existence with a
pre-Convulsion anachronism dictating terms to him.

Printed in the United States
52982LVS00002B/27

9 781587 154478